EVERYTHING CHANGED AFTER THAT

25 Women, 25 Stories

EMBASSY BOOKS

www.embassybooks.in

Published in India by:
Embassy Book Distributors
120, Great Western Building,
Maharashtra Chamber of Commerce Lane,
Fort, Mumbai 400 023, India
Tel: (+9122) -30967415, 22819546
Email: info@embassybooks.in
www.embassybooks.in

ISBN: 978-93-89995-50-3

Cover Design by Sonal Churi

Layout and typesetting by Sonal Churi &
Gangaram Dhuri (Brand Soul Creations)

CONTENTS

FOREWORD

My job as editor-in-chief at Embassy Books gives me ample opportunity to read all kinds of works from all over the world. Being an avid reader and an author myself, I fully appreciate how difficult it is to write a good short story. It requires a special skill – that of containing the narration within a limited number of words while outlining the essence of each character and skillfully weaving the plot to a satisfactory conclusion. A great short story navigates you through the fluid and transient world of the author's imagination in just a few pages, arousing your emotions, surprising and mesmerising you at times, and landing you back safely to where you started, but with an internal shift. A great story touches your heart and compels you to ponder over what you read.

When *eShe* magazine held a short story writing contest for women in collaboration with Embassy Books, the response was overwhelming, with submissions from 216 women across the nation. Each story allowed us to dive deep into the hearts and minds of these women writers. I was amazed at the creativity, imagination, expression and passion with which the stories were written. It was evident that each writer had so much to offer to the world. They came from various walks of life – from students and doctors to social workers and engineers.

Each and every story we received was unique and thought-provoking in its own way. It was a tough call to select the twenty-five stories that would finally make their way into this book. But that is what competition is all about. The work is often evaluated on the basis of certain parameters. However, the selection of the winning stories does not make the other stories inferior in any way.

After a lot of deliberation, twenty-five stories were selected by the panel of judges, which included bestselling author Preeti Shenoy, Aekta Kapoor, the founder of *eShe*, and myself. There was a common thread weaving these stories together – the thread of womanhood and that of a life-changing experience. Each story had a bottom line – everything changed after that. This also made an appropriate title for this anthology.

There could not have been a better person to compile and edit these stories than Aekta Kapoor, who has had an illustrious career as an editor having interviewed thousands of women for various magazines she had been associated with. I have known Aekta for almost a decade now and have been witness to her passionate contribution to the field of women's empowerment, which is now directed towards successfully running a women's magazine that amplifies women's voices and stories of our shared humanity. The tagline at Embassy Books is *Life-Changing Books*. We feel privileged to bring to our readers this anthology that is completely in tune with our ethos.

Get ready to immerse yourself in this captivating collection of short stories that will surprise you, shock you, make you cry and laugh, but in the end will leave you with a changed perspective towards life.

Aruna Joshi
Author and Editor-in-chief,
Embassy Books, Mumbai

PREFACE

What are the stories that Indian women would write if they were given total freedom to express their thoughts and experiences? What are the dreams and fantasies they would share? What make-believe worlds would they imagine?

When *eShe* magazine launched a nationwide short-story contest for women writers in the midst of the Covid lockdown in 2020, these were some of the questions on our mind. Seeking twenty-five stories to be published by Embassy Books as an anthology, we were taken aback by the 216 we received within days. That was over 400,000 words to be compiled, read and judged within four weeks to make it to our promised deadline to our contestants.

The judges for the contest naturally had a huge task at hand. All of us would later agree: our expectations were surpassed, our minds stretched, our eyes opened a little bit more.

So what are the stories Indian women tell? They tell of myths and reality, love and hatred, pain and ambition, shame and success. There were stories of being oppressed by families and husbands, and others of breaking out and finding hope. There were tales of extramarital affairs and finding one's school flame in adulthood, of nasty divorces and custody battles. There were glimpses into rural Indian preoccupations and patriarchy, of India's natural beauty and the power of its spirituality and folklore.

There were stories of misunderstandings between mothers and daughters, fathers and sons, husbands and wives. There were stories of reconciliation with old lovers, of waking up to same-sex love, of starting over a second time. There were sagas of being forced into prostitution, committing foeticide or being tempted into accepting bribes. There were several stories of finding validation despite challenges: a schoolteacher earns respect from her abusive in-laws when she wins acclaim for introducing online systems to her rural school during lockdown; a mother who loses her child and husband in a freak accident finds a new purpose teaching orphans in a village.

There were touching journeys of finding self-respect despite living in an unjust world – a farm worker and single mother finds the courage to ward off her lewd employer who frequently forces her into sex. A girl with a learning disability faces up to the daily humiliation she faces in school and learns to accept herself. An absent-minded homemaker, whose friends find her vacuous and pampered, finds a new mission during the lockdown and takes up training to become a special educator. There were also stories peppered with tongue-in-cheek humour, and thrilling roller-coasters of mystery or crime.

Interestingly, though this was a fiction-writing contest, many of the contestants – including some in this book – drew their stories from real-life events. Winners were chosen based on various factors but one thing unites the tales in this collection: they wouldn't leave our minds long after we read them.

Having met and interviewed thousands of women over my career in women's magazines and now running my own, I have encountered all kinds of stories of Indian women. But no matter how many I listen and read, they never cease to surprise me.

It's hard enough to write to a theme within a short deadline, but it's harder to put your labour of love up for judging, lay it bare to scrutiny, and leave yourself vulnerable to rejection. Though these twenty-five writers came out on top, all the women who sent in their stories are winners to me.

Aekta Kapoor
Editor and Publisher,
eShe magazine,
New Delhi, India

SKYWARD BOUND

Arti Jain

I always loved turnstile doors. You know, the kind in office buildings and banks and other important places. You have to make up your mind about which direction you are going, in or out, and then just go for it. The undecided can go round and round forever.

Life is like that too. No one knows that better than me because I take forever in life's turnstile doors. I can't make up my mind about anything. The more important the decision, the more it freezes me into inaction. This is what happened when there was talk about finding a groom for me. I did not react in time to say that I did not want to get married. At least not to Harjeet, who insisted on being called Harry, because everyone in London called him that.

At college, I secretly stole glances at Imtiaz. He always sat by the window in his class and when he wasn't frowning at his books, he looked out at the sky. Just below which I stood, deliberately taking my own sweet time to put my cycle on its stand and lock it and pick up my bag and adjust my *dupatta*, until his eyes descended from the clouds to where I was. I don't know if it was a thought he had picked off the skies or it was the sight of me, but he always smiled. And he always pushed back his hair from his forehead. At that moment I felt a sudden need to get out of there as fast as possible.

Harry and I were to be married in a week because he had to be back in London before the start of the Christmas sale at his store. After that first time when he came with his parents to "see" me, he came to our house often. He sat in the courtyard with my father and ate everything that was brought out. Sometimes he'd walk to a corner and talk in hushed tones on the phone with his family and then give instructions to mine. My father, as tough and unshakable as the neem tree in the courtyard, turned as pliant as vine when Harry spoke to him. My mother was an unrecognisable mess, a mix of giddy happiness and breathless panic. She packed stacks of sweets in the new shiny suitcase. She fought with the tailor to get my suits stitched in time. She unpacked and packed my bags again and again. I heard murmurs about the loan my father took from his office. I saw mother and him going to the bank and returning with all the jewellery from the locker. Everything she owned was in a small old black purse that she had tucked tightly under her armpit. The few times that Harry and I were left alone, so we could get to know each other, he talked nonstop about his store, his car, his house. When he spoke he waved his arms a lot and when the sun caught his golden watch, you could see fireflies on the courtyard walls in the afternoon. He asked me if I had a tongue in my mouth or if I just stared at walls like a cow. I cleared my throat and started to tell him about my college and friends. He looked at me with his head tilted. "Did they teach you to cook some good chicken at this college? More useful," he sniggered. Then he picked up his phone and started to look through his messages. I didn't reply nor continue what I was saying. He dialed a number and walked away to talk. When he wasn't talking on the phone, he was staring into the phone. Harry never looked up at the sky.

On the day of the wedding, I woke up with a start. There was a racket outside. I looked out of the bedroom window into the courtyard. There were familiar faces and strangers. Some men were putting up a *shamiana* in the courtyard, one of my uncles was shouting instructions to the *halwais*, father was giving our house help a piece of his mind, my brother and his friends were trying to hang a string of lights from the terrace. My younger cousins were practising their dance steps. I shut the window and sat down on my bed again. Everyone says that the wedding day is the happiest day in a girl's life. Then why did I feel so numb? I am no fool. I know this is the best thing that could have happened to me. A life of comfort abroad was better than the best I could hope for here. The farthest I could dream of was to be a schoolteacher. I liked that thought but then again, if I lived abroad maybe I could help my family with some money and have my brother move abroad too. I felt better just thinking about it. My mother was calling out. I got up to get ready.

The wedding itself didn't take very long. Afterwards, Harry and I were made to sit down to eat lunch next to each other. He would sometimes lean close to my ear and whisper jokes that I didn't understand, his voice thick with half-chewed food. I knew they were jokes because he would laugh non-stop for several minutes afterwards. The more confused I looked, the longer he laughed.

It was late at night when we left for the airport. Harry's parents were staying back to spend time with their relatives, so it was just us. I sat in the backseat, next to Harry. He fell asleep soon, his arms and legs spread across the back seat like a pinned rat in the biology lab. I looked out into the darkness and cried all the way. For my parents whom I wouldn't see again for a long time. For my friends Shabbo and Rani, who hugged me and cried so much they got their snot on my *dupatta* (that made us smile a little too). For my college professor who tried to talk my mother into letting me finish my degree but gave up when I told her I didn't want her to call my mother because it upset her. For all the things I had to leave behind because Harry said it costs a lot of money if the luggage was even two-hundred-and-fifty grams more than what's allowed.

And for Imtiaz, whom I saw on my last morning at college. I had spotted him from afar and quickly hid myself behind a wall. He was standing by the cycle stand. He seemed to be waiting for someone, looking at his wrist-watch again and again. I turned back and pedalled home as fast as I could. As the memory rose, I squeezed my eyes shut hard to get the image out of my brain forever.

The taxi stopped. Harry jumped out and told the driver to put our luggage on a wheeled cart. I stepped out into the roar of cars, horns and people shouting. I felt like throwing up. Harry asked for me for my passport. I had put it in the inside pocket of my purse. My hands were clammy and my fingers were slipping, unable to open the zipper. With one sweep, Harry snatched the bag, ripped open the zip and pulled out the passport. He tossed the bag back in my hands and muttered something in English. I didn't have to understand the words to feel their heat. Harry was striding towards the gate, tickets and passports in hand. He turned once and gestured to me to follow. I hung my handbag on my shoulder and pushed the trolley to the gate, careful not to let the suitcases slide off.

The airport was a vast cavernous belly of a giant whale and people were like chewed-up creatures floating in it. I was trying to keep pace with Harry and every time he dipped out of sight my heart skipped a beat. Just when I thought I had caught up with him, he stopped suddenly.

"Stay here," he told me, jabbing his finger at the floor. Before I could nod, he was gone. It was a relief, not having to push the mountain of suitcases and to just stand for a bit and look around.

That's when I saw her first. She was dressed like me, in a bright *salwar* suit and pretty gold jewellery, a white purse hanging from her shoulder. Her face was turned away and she was looking towards the long line a few feet away. A small girl was clinging to her leg and staring at me. Something about the child's wide-eyed gaze and open mouth made me smile. She immediately hid behind her mother's leg, only to peep out again in a second. I put my palm on my eyes and then peeped out at her. She broke into a laugh. Her mother looked at me too.

"You are very naughty," the mother patted her daughter's head in mock rebuke and smiled at me.

Just then a big suitcase fell down in front of us. At first I thought it was from my pile but it wasn't. A tall man in a blue tracksuit had flung a suitcase on the floor between the woman and me. He was hissing with anger. He flung open the suitcase and pulled the woman down by her elbow towards it.

"Take this nonsense out NOW... stupid woman. Everything is

overweight!" he was almost shouting.

The woman was grabbing things as he flung them out. An old metal box came out first, then a hand-knitted sweater, polythene bags tied with rubber bands, a cheap plastic toy, a photo frame.

The woman was red in the face, her *dupatta* had fallen off her chest to the floor. She was apologising to her husband, trying to make him stop. "Uncouth villagers like you... six hundred times you travel from India, each time you bring garbage and expect me to pay for it! What can I expect for marrying a bloody sweeper's daughter?"

The woman looked up for a second. Her eyes caught mine and were locked for what seemed like a long time. But it wasn't that long after all. She looked away, embarrassed. People were walking around the stuff on the floor, trying to not look at the drama unfolding at their feet. A kindly looking lady in uniform was telling the man to calm down and move everything to a corner. The little girl was wailing, trying to grab her mother's arm.

My chest was heaving with fear and anger and shame. I was that woman. Or would be soon. Her eyes had drilled a hole in my heart and every lie I had told myself flowed out of it in an unstoppable gush. And with it, something in me collapsed to pieces.

I saw Harry gesturing to me from the line. I was looking at him but it was as if my limbs were bolted to the floor. I saw Harry leave the line and come towards me really fast. He was frowning with irritation.

Before he could say anything I turned to face him.

"I can't come with you, Harry," I said. "This was a mistake... my mistake."

"Have you lost your mind, you idi..."

I didn't wait to hear the rest of what he had to say. I turned away. I was walking... walking faster...

"Stop," someone said behind me.

I didn't stop. I couldn't stop. My heartbeat and the sound of my heels on the floor were one.

I was running.

"Madam... Madam... you can't go out this way!" a man called out.

 I threw myself at the turnstile door and pushed my way out.

Outside, the sun was about to come out and the air was cool and pink. I stopped to look up and the sky spread itself out for me to fly.

Arti Jain studied New Media at Stanford University, holds an MFA in cinema from San Francisco State University and an MA in mass communications from Jamia Millia Islamia. She has worn various hats – as associate producer for an Emmy Award-winning TV series, co-founder of one of India's early online bookstores, and even a storytelling coach. In 2020, Arti combined her three loves – theatre, radio and books – to produce her podcast StoryJam, where she narrates texts from Hindi and Urdu literature.

A SEASONAL QUIDDITY

Manisha Sahoo

A blinding star was attached to the glass. Its rays dipped and differed, shrouding the outside world in golden mystery nonetheless. Its warmth, though, was quite comforting.

Between it and Kerry, I believed I had found where I wanted to belong.

She dragged an armchair across the tiled floor, screeches bouncing off the walls, until it faced my place of perch. A footstool appeared between us overnight, and in the days that followed, Kerry often sat in the armchair, using the footstool for its original purpose or as a table, as she saw fit.

"This new place is... lovely, isn't it?" She sunk into the cushion and closed her eyes, letting out air through her lips. "I could get used to it, ha, ha," she laughed.

She drifted off to sleep soon and I revelled in the warmth rushing in through the open window. This was the perfect temperature. A little hotter, or a little colder, and it would be bothersome. I knew well enough how often and how quick temperatures were susceptible to change. While these large mammals might not discern the minute differences, to me, to us, they mattered.

If I was not pampered as I was, I would perhaps be more adaptable. But I found it easier to ignore the 'ifs' because the present felt all too blissful to not cherish.

Kerry showed up every day before sunset for those initial days. If it was at a time I was drifting to sleep, she would apologise and laugh and apologise again, giving me water before wishing me a good night.

Otherwise, she talked. About many things. Her family, her Mama, her sister Vera, her office, her travels, the strangers she ran into. I did not understand a lot of it.

Like how someone in her workplace made her laugh. I saw her laugh quite freely while talking, so I did not understand how someone could make her do something she was so accustomed to anyway.

And then when I thought she was talking to me, I found her not looking at me, while sitting across from me. There were also times when she did not talk at all. She chuckled on her own, smiled, grinned and laughed; all the while her head would be bowed and her eyes endowed with an unnatural glow. I would feel left out. Why were there so many secret jokes I was not a part of?

Days would be lonely when she was working, especially the ones when she worked longer than usual. The armchair without her in it looked ugly. Glossy wicker with a striped cushion. The footstool matched the patterns.

I tried counting the stripes once, until I realised I did not know how to count. I know *one* minute, *one* second was a single finger, because Kerry lifted it anytime a strange ringing interrupted our talk time. More often than not, the ringing belonged to the same thing that set her face aglow. I decided I hated that thing.

What was the point of it anyway? Tch. It was grey and gloomy-looking. Sadness dripped from its edges and nothing else.

Always. Interrupting.

Worst was when it would send Kerry scrambling out of the room. Did it not understand her relaxation schedule? How dumb was it?

One such ringing later, a smiling Kerry froze in time. I could have sworn everything else was moving ahead in that chasm of stillness, but Kerry did not. Not for a long while. She looked like a rooted tree trunk, no longer bearing any leaves. Stagnant as death itself.

She left again like before, but something was different this time. She moved slower, her feet dragged and her face had changed colour. I did not know humans did that. I did not know they were seasonal like nature, like us.

The house became quiet after that. I noticed Kerry only a few times, leaving the room just as I was waking up. The shape of her back grew familiar to me and I did not like it. And a strange noise echoed through the house, day in, day out. I did not like that either. Like water forcing its way through a hollow reed, clogged with weeds.

The sun, when it smiled, glowed the same, when it raged hurt the same, and the window remained as defenceless a barrier for me as always. None of them mattered to me more than the armchair that sat empty. I could see the wicker was not without flaw either. It jutted out in spots, and its sheen had chipped away in places. The cushion had sunk. I could tell.

That must be why Kerry did not like sitting there anymore. Everything in this room must make her feel uncomfortable.

Because of the useless window and the hopeless cushion, I lost my precious hours of talk time with my only friend. If only I could change either or both. But what could I do?

One scorching morning, because the sun found it funny to rain down all its heat on a battered soul like mine, I woke up feeling thirsty. Kerry had not been here yet. I brightened up a little. Could it be that I woke up in time to catch a glimpse of her face for once?

Perhaps – perhaps she would stay if she knew I was awake. Oh, would that not be grand! I could imagine the bountiful drops of heaven making a dance on the earth! The whole world would rejoice and come alive!

Even the dumb thing would not be as dumb anymore.

And so I waited.

I could not tell the time, but the moon told me it was night. When it next greeted me, I was parched and tired. The loneliness, the lack of water, was getting to me.

Where was Kerry? She never left my side for so long without informing. Where was she? Where was her laugh? I would even take the weird choking noise if it meant she was in the house.

I missed Kerry.

I missed water.

I missed being cared for.

I lost count of how many days went by. I could not count anyway, but things were too fuzzy to make sense. I had not been nourished in ages. I had not moved anywhere, I had stayed in the same little room, soaking in the energy of the golden orb in all its glory and might. It had me beaten and ill.

I could not imagine feeling better from this.

I did not register anything till limbs vaguely lingered in my vision. Voices I did not recognise – because they were not Kerry's – spoke in broken sentences. Kerry spoke this way too, when she was enveloped in a mirth she could not control. But this was different.

The intruders were different, their manner of speaking spread dread through me. What were they planning?

I could not quite comprehend them... it looked like the end of the road for me...

Except, a cold trickle of water caressed my parched leaves and I lapped up the little dose of the miraculous elixir I had been craving for so long. More... I needed more... how could I tell them, whoever they were?

**

"It's almost dead, sweetie. Do you really want to –?"

He stopped when her shoulders stiffened. "I... I can't... I can't let anything else die... not of Mama's or Kerry's..."

Vera could not control the trembling that wracked her whole body. Comforting arms wrapped around her and she leaned into them. Tears poured out without restraint, blurring the wicker armchair and the cushioned footstool in front of her. Kerry must have loved to sit there and enjoy some quiet time.

Just like Mama.

**

When hands clasped around me and picked me up, I had too many questions unanswered and no way to ask. I did not even know yet whether I would survive any longer. Were they taking me away? Could they even keep me even half as healthy as Kerry did? She was diligent and sweet and spoke to me. None of her guests or acquaintances engaged with me.

A little more water and my vision cleared. I noticed the facial features of the one who held me up. The eyes, nose, shape of the face were familiar. Similar kind with different lips and hair had graced the armchair and given me company for a long time. Where was that one? Why was I with a Kerry-lookalike?

Maybe I should not have wondered. Maybe some questions are better kept hidden away so they could not be bleached into the faded colours of a cruel truth.

"You may not know me, but I know you well. My name is Vera. I'm Kerry's older sister. She sent me your photo when you were a wee little thing, when Mama picked you out for her. She gave me one too, different kind. Our grown-up presents, moving-out-of-home presents, being-independent presents. Mama... she..."

The lady would not speak of them again for days. She brought me to a new place, put me beside another of my kind and introduced us. I stayed sickly for many more turns of the sun and the moon. The other one talked in the meantime. Chatterbox.

It knew everything. How Kerry and Vera's Mama suffered a fatal heart attack. How Kerry could not make it to the funeral but she was determined to attend the other rites without fail. How she had applied for leave that day and had left the office early to come home and pack. How she got into a road accident while returning from work...

It always trailed off as if I would know to fill the blanks. I did not. I could not. Nothing it said made sense. Nothing it expected me to know beforehand made sense. What happened after that? Where did Kerry go?

I waited for her to turn up in the new place. I missed the scrappy little armchair with its striped cushion. Fine, I would even say I missed the footstool-slash-table.

I missed the sunlight dancing on the polished portions of the wicker, springing stars in Kerry's eyes and teeth when she laughed, illuminating her whole face.

I missed Kerry sitting across from me, her legs folded under her weight, and her arms knowing no rest while she talked.

Wherever Kerry was, I wondered if she missed me too.

**

"Kerry, dear, come here. I think one of these would be perfect for your new place."

"Isn't that different from what you gave to Vera?"

"Yes, because both of you are different. Vera would never water them regularly, and you would."

"Very true. So you think one of these would last long?"

"What do you take me for? Don't I maintain a gorgeous garden at home? It's just you girls who grew up and decided to leave me alone!"

"Aw, Mama! We still love you, you know that! And I promise to come in every weekend!"

"That's two days in a week only. And it will only be at the start, I know that very well. Before long, it will turn into Sundays only. Then, work would be all you would think about, doing overtime, doing the weekends too. And then you'd be too tired to travel. And before you know it, I'll be gone and you won't have an obligation for the weekend anyway."

"Hush, Mama! We still have to travel the world together, remember? You cannot think about leaving me without doing that first. I won't allow you."

"*Sure*, dear. Now, shut up with your nonsense and pick one of these."

"This one, then. I just feel like it belongs with me."

"You and your absurd reasons."

"Ha, ha."

*Based in Bhubaneswar, Odisha, **Manisha Sahoo** got a Bachelor's degree as an engineer, followed it up with a short stint in an IT company, and then did her Master's in English. Since then, she has won several fiction-writing contests, been published in an anthology, and has received an honorable mention in L. Ron Hubbard's Writers of the Future.*

THE KARMA SEED

Nina Krishna Warrier

I loved spending my summer holidays at my *tharavadu*, ancestral home, at Neeliyad in Kerala.

In the early seventies, Neeliyad was a sleepy hamlet. The nearest post office was the Kumaranellur post office, about a kilometre away from Neeliyad to the east. It was also connected to Anakkara in the north by a dusty road flanked on either side by paddy fields. Our house was about a hundred metres down Anakkara Road.

I found, much later, that Anakkara's claim to fame was that it was the *tharavadu* of the internationally acclaimed Indian classical dancer, choreographer and teacher, Mrinalini Sarabhai. In 2016, Mrinalini's 86-year-old cousin, Malini Achuthan, told a reporter of *The Hindu* newspaper, "Although she was born and brought up outside Kerala, Mrinalini had strong affection for Anakkara and the 120-year-old Vadakkath Tharavadu." Vadakkathu Tharavadu was also the birthplace of Mrinalini's elder sister, Captain Lakshmi Sahgal, who led the Rani of Jhansi Regiment in the Indian National Army of Subhas Chandra Bose.

Ours was a simple one-bedroom thatched cottage. The house didn't have electricity. Towards evening, my *valliamma* (literally translated from Malayalam as 'elder mother'; she was my father's elder sister), a widow with no children, used to clean the soot off the glass covers of both the *raanthal*, a small lamp, and the *paanees*, the larger more sophisticated variety, and fill them with kerosene. I used to like it when *valliamma* would light a *vilakku, pooja* lamp, come out holding it in her two hands to the verandah where my father, mother and I would be sitting indulging in general chatter, and pronounce, "*Deepam*". After about an hour and a half we would all move to the kitchen, our shadows dancing in the flickering lights of the lanterns, and partake of our simple dinner.

There was a small *parambu*, the land adjoining the house, populated with coconut trees, areca nut trees, papaya trees, cashew nut trees, mango trees, and flowering shrubs like hibiscus, *mogra* and more. Occasionally, in the mornings, I used to collect flowers for *valliamma* who would go to the family temple next to the pond, a stone's throw away, and string a garland for Lord Krishna every day. In my childish enthusiasm, I even accompanied her a couple of times. But my need to sleep was stronger than stringing a garland for Krishna.

In the *parambu* there was this mango tree. It was called *ottu maavu*, grafted mango tree. It had a few low-slung branches. In spite of my parents' protestations, I would climb the tree regularly. A couple of times I scraped my knees while climbing down. But, of course, that didn't deter me.

One of my favourite branches on the mango tree snaked across the thatched roof of the house and had a fork of sorts. I would climb the tree and perch myself there. I liked that top-of-the-world feeling. The tree was laden with mangoes in the summer. The fruit wasn't particularly sweet but I used to enjoy it all the same.

One day, since the branch posed a threat to the roof of the house, my *valliamma*, after consulting with my father, decided to chop off the branch. I found out about it in the evening and I got angry. I protested. I said that it was my branch and no way would I allow it to be cut. Everyone ignored me. I slept fitfully that night.

I got up early next morning. I was surly. I didn't acknowledge my parents or my *valliamma*. To my horror, I saw Klari, the farm hand, with an axe in his hand.

Klari smiled at me and said, "*Kutty*, kid, I am going to chop off your favourite branch." I don't know what came over me then. I started bawling loudly. I quickly ran to the tree and before anyone knew what was happening, I was perched on my favourite branch. Everyone was stunned. First they cajoled me, then they scolded me, and later my parents threatened to hand me over to the police. But I stuck to my guns. This impasse continued for an hour.

In the end, exasperated, the elders relented. The branch would stay. I was happy and climbed down.

To celebrate my triumph I plucked a ripe mango from the tree.

"Aren't you eating it?" my mother asked.

"I'll have it tomorrow," I replied.

"But we are going to Valanchery tomorrow," my father piped in.

"So what?" I asked. "I'll carry it with me to eat in the car."

"You'll spoil the whole car," mother interjected. "And your dress too."

I objected, "I'll make sure the juice doesn't ruin my dress."

"Stubborn girl," my mother said to no one in particular. "Always having it your way. But remember, no spoiling the dress."

The next day, after breakfast, we set out for Valanchery, about 20 kilometres north of Neeliyad, in a hired Ambassador car. First we drove in a westerly direction to Edappal Chungam, Edappal Junction that is, and then turned north towards Valanchery. We passed coconut groves and paddy fields, and thatched houses with kids minus their shirts waving to us. I waved back a few times.

It was a pleasant enough journey in the rickety Ambassador. My father was seated in the front next to the driver. My mother and I were sitting on the back seat. I dozed off ten minutes into the journey. About an hour later I woke up with a start. I was disoriented. And I wanted to pee.

Mother tried to shush me. But after another five minutes, I couldn't hold it anymore. I told my father. He looked at the driver. The driver said in Malayalam that half a kilometre ahead there was a lonely spot of sorts, *Kutty* could relieve herself there. He stopped the car there soon after.

I got out of the car with my mother. She carried a *kooja*, brassware with a lid that could be screwed down, filled with water with her. I relieved myself by the roadside. My mother poured some water out of the *kooja* for me to wash hands, which I did cursorily.

Now that I had relieved myself, I started to feel hungry. I told my mother that I wanted to eat the mango I'd plucked the previous day. She yelled to my father to fetch the mango from the car. My father got the mango and gave it to me. But I could see that he was irritated. I think fathers are creatures of habit. They don't like their routines disturbed. Mothers, on the other hand, are more adaptable and improvising.

I surveyed the land in front of me. It was scenic in its own way. My gaze travelled along the slope that plunged into a valley some hundred feet below. There was a sizeable rock standing sentinel over the valley. Before my mother could say *Kutty*, I ran towards the rock, scampered up, and laughed looking down at her. My mother shouted after me to come down immediately.

I said, "Let me finish the mango. I'll come down then."

My mother yelled to my father, "Look, what your daughter is doing!"

My father looked angry. But he must have thought, better not disturb this mischievous girl. God alone knows what she's capable of.

So I sat on the rock and finished eating the mango. It felt like some kind of victory to me. For some reason, the mango tasted sweet too. I was about to wipe the juice of the mango that was on my hands on my dress when mother shouted, "Don't spoil your dress!"

Little did mother know that I also had other plans.

I clambered down the rock and called out to my mother, "Just five minutes. I want to bury this mango seed in the ground next to this rock. Will it grow, *amma*?"

My mother replied impatiently, "It may or may not. You finish it fast and come. We are getting late."

I used a stick lying close by to dig the earth. Surprisingly, the ground was soft. I made a hole about half a foot deep, buried the seed and traipsed towards my mother.

My mother gave me a small pinch on my arm. It really didn't hurt me but I looked at my dad rather balefully and pretended to cry. My father scooped me up in his arms and we wended our way back to the car.

We visited my maternal uncle, had lunch at his house, and returned home by nightfall.

**

Some eighteen years passed since my last visit to Neeliyad when I'd thrown the tantrum to prevent the chopping of the mango tree branch. Somehow, that incident stayed with me. Now, here I was, again, driving with my husband of one year, Anoop, to visit my uncle at Valanchery.

Valliamma had passed away eight years earlier. After her demise, the family members divided her assets among themselves. My father opted for cash as he was employed in Bombay (it hadn't become Mumbai as yet). My cousin – my maternal uncle's son – bought the Neeliyad land and built a house on the same premises. He lived there with his wife and four-year old son. My cousin's father, my uncle, continued to live in Valanchery at his wife's house.

Anoop was driving my cousin's Maruti Zen. I was sitting in the front with him. The car's radio was playing Bollywood numbers.

"It's nice to get out of the house and hit the road in the morning," I said.

"Absolutely," replied Anoop. "There's less traffic too at this hour."

"Why don't you play some Rafi songs," I asked.

"Ah, there we go again. Rafi versus Kishore Kumar."

"Rafi singing for Shammi Kapoor. That's the ultimate."

"Darling, my vote still goes for Kishore."

We both burst out laughing.

We were happily married and very much in love. We enjoyed this playful banter.

I noticed that there was quite a bit of traffic on the road. More importantly, I realised that the drivers were rash. The local government-run buses, nicknamed *aana*, Malayalam for elephant, looked upon the narrow roads as a race track. It was always wise to give them a wide berth. I also noticed a lot of tanker-lorries and private buses plying on the road. Kerala was changing. Must be the Gulf money, I thought.

Kishore Kumar was singing *Zindagi ek safar hai suhana...*

Anoop looked to his left and said, "What a beautiful valley!"

I too turned reflexively to my left and said excitedly, "Wow! And look at that mango tree in bloom."

He turned left again to look at the tree when he saw a huge truck coming straight at him. He swerved. The car veered off the road and slipped down the slope.

The Maruti skidded downhill, Anoop trying desperately to stop it. Then it came to a sudden halt as it got wedged between the rock and the fully grown, sturdy mango tree.

*Former copywriter **Nina Krishna Warrier** is now a full-time homemaker and amateur author. Based in Mumbai, she loves meeting new people, travelling to new places, and is a fan of seventies' and eighties' music. She goes by her mother's advice, to "enjoy and endure", and says her biggest strengths are her daughter, husband, brother, sister-in-law and nieces.*

AKHILA

Preetha Vasan

The sky turns a deep purple. It is a good two-hour wait for our dinner guest. Our narrow balcony dazzles hibiscus-mauve under the evening light, because I have washed it six times since afternoon in honour of the guest. Amma is done with her cooking. She stacks the curries into her small kitchen ladder, wipes her ceramic cutlery for the hundredth time and frowns at her counter top. It is a gleaming white, outshining its own record of weeknight-pearl greys and weekend-crispy creams. Amma attacks it afresh with more of her hot water-soap formula. It would be futile to tell Amma that this is the best her twenty-year-old counter top, flanked by cracking tiles, will look. She would still scrub it, wrench out the crease, and wash the turmeric stains. Amma loves cleaning the counter top, like the way she loves scrubbing windows, electrical switches, bathroom floors and door knobs. Maybe because she cannot clean the clutter within, she does her best without. And now that the comet-guest plans to appear on the seven p.m. horizon, Amma pesters me and the house into a hospital-like spotlessness.

Since the time Appa left us for that writer woman, we have never had guests. Since the time Appa left us for that writer woman, Akhila has ensured we never had guests. Not that we, Amma and

I, cared, because Akhila gave us plenty of other things to worry about. Guests were hardly top of the list.

I was five the year Appa left us, guests stopped visiting, and Akhila, my elder sister, changed. First her grades dropped, then her temper tantrums escalated, and pretty soon everything went wrong between her and Amma. Their shouting matches would echo through our tiny apartment, down our building's dull ill-lit stairway, through nosey neighbours' doors and windows. That's why people, I assumed, stopped dropping in at our "nut house". Akhila gave Amma the hardest time. In case I had not guessed that by my eighth year, Amma whispered it to me as she crawled under our double-size cotton bed sheets every night.

Akhila is seven years older than me. These years between us are a chasm of incomprehension, because for a long time I never understood my sister. I blamed her for Amma's six a.m. wrath and my black-and-blue bruises from Amma's stinging raps. And Akhila, I thought, blamed Amma for Appa's desertion, and our middleclass poverty. I have never asked her about these conjectures of mine. I just made them over the years.

Sometimes I wonder why he left. Amma is pretty in an Amma-way, I suppose. She is smart and funny – the latter side of her, however, is hardly visible these days. But Akhila must have known why he left, she was twelve then. If she had not actually known, she must have definitely figured it all out, because by the time I hit twelve I had figured out, or thought I did, quite a bit myself – about my sister and my miscalculations regarding several things – specifically because I replayed in my head, several times, a Diwali bonfire, two days after my seventh birthday and the oath my sister made me take, once we both had spat three times inside our palms, because I had insisted that is how we seal our promises. Akhila must have known why he left, and fought with Amma for other reasons that had nothing to do with Appa. A deep gut-level loyalty told me Akhila was unfair to Amma, who was struggling and straddling her many odd jobs to manage our basic luxuries. But when you are twelve going on thirteen, full of the acne-and-pimple wrath of an adolescent, stifled by curfew time and convinced that you are a grown up, gut-level loyalties take a walk.

I was certain Amma had been wrong all along about Akhila. My sister, I strongly believed, was a free spirit, who Amma with all her rigidities, could not tame. I loved everything about my sister, simply because Amma abhorred them all: her Iron Maiden tattoo down her long and spindly back; her gothic makeup, which she liberally tried on me; the piercings (especially the navel one, about which Amma has no idea) and the night she came stoned, throwing up all over our withering, almost-straw, jute doormat.

Eventually, I reckoned, everything about Akhila is conflict, debate and sometimes dialogue, because our mother made the wrong decision about surrendering her life to a man she had hardly known. And for my sister, once Appa trashed us like old newspaper, the rationale was pretty simple. If one decision can go so wrong, how can any decision ever be right? Hence Akhila never made up her mind about anything, and would not allow anyone else to make it for her. Apart from her weekly shouting matches with Amma, who unfortunately is frighteningly decisive, or other frequent nerve-wracking occasions – like the night she shaved her head bald because Amma asked her about the one-month-long pending college applications, and the days we ran around our narrow neighbourhood lanes trying to find her after one of her meltdowns – Akhila was no trouble at all.

Growing up with my sister resolved a lot of things for me, like choices and emotional intelligence. The first were super easy to make and the second a quicksilver achievement. I guess Akhila did that to me. Not directly. But there were so many layers to resolve with everything Akhila did, the straight path came to me easily. No ambivalence. No dillydallying. And when thinking becomes too hard, I hand over matters to Amma, who nevertheless worries for all of us, three times over. Unlike Akhila.

One year, Akhila was all about medical colleges and entrance exams, which came to zilch. The next year, amidst standard Akhila disappearances and Amma's increasingly frequent migraines, we had elaborate debates about universities and colleges. Finally, Akhila shoved everything and went and did a fashion-technology course. That's the time Amma gave our in-house pressure cooker a complex and Akhila vacated temporarily to live with her best friend, Meghna. After the steam abated, Akhila moved back, followed by periods of silence menacingly noisier and somehow more ominous than all the shouting episodes of the past.

Over the months, Akhila got a job as a fashion designer's assistant and kept threatening to move out, but thankfully never did. Our lives moved on at its usual mundane pace. Amma and Akhila spoke less and hence quarrelled less and our apartment has turned a strange quiet.

A couple of weeks ago, on a quiet Saturday evening, Akhila turned twenty-three. I was happy I finally understood my sister. This grand achievement came crashing down once she announced, while I was stuffing her with the cardboard-hard cake we had baked, her engagement. Amma and I were taken aback, to say the least. If there had been debates and contemplations, they had all been in Akhila's head. I never heard of any. Neither had Amma, with whom she seldom spoke, anyway. Did we miss the drama? Not exactly. However, I felt a tad betrayed. She could have told me! I know everything about her. Including the navel piercing! Plus I had never thought she was the dating kind, or worse the marrying kind. Of course, she is twenty-three and should be "settled" and all that, as our neighbour Meena auntie insists. Yet I cannot imagine my sister as someone's "wife". I was not jealous, but certainly curious to meet the bloke who was smitten by my mercurial sister, about whom Amma and my thwarted ego abstained from asking. Within a couple of days, Amma thawed and insisted, despite Akhila's scowls and grimaces, that she introduce us to her fiancé.

When such a fiancé is a guest for dinner, there are no cutting corners. Amma has given up her plastered look since the announcement and revoked our odd chips and cola luxuries through the week to accommodate the grand dinner. Akhila, who never cares about food, told Amma not to bother and even suggested her strange mix-and-match menu. Amma, a thoroughbred purist, nodded and did not demur, then went about cooking her best recipes, as if Akhila had made no suggestions at all.

Amma plans to serve the dinner in the balcony I have cleaned six times. I'm not sure if that's a great idea. Meena auntie's plastic Neelkamal tables and chairs – wiped to their nascent whiteness, rubbing legs and edges with each other – look crowded in our narrow balcony. Amma says it will work if Akhila and her fiancé eat first. I smother a giggle, imagining Akhila's reaction when Amma announces this very ceremonial idea. Well, we certainly cannot serve him food at our counter top, or the sofa, which is where we normally eat, so I guess Neelkamal will have to do.

Seven p.m. It is time. I hope this guy does not follow Akhila's version of the Indian standard time because I am hungry and cannot wait another two hours, which is when the pair will probably arrive. But the doorbell rings as our grandfather clock lets out its slow mournful peals. Amma bolts out of her chair. Clearly, she had not expected this punctuality, either.

Amma looks nervous. I reach the door first, my curiosity tottering on the brink of an explosion.

Akhila fidgets with her fringe and shuffles in her loose baggy jeans, always a size bigger than her frail self. I am about to ask, "Where's your fiancé?", when I spot the tall, lanky frame behind my sister.

But it's just Meghna beaming at me. Does Amma know Akhila has invited her best friend too? We have only four Neelkamal chairs and a narrow balcony.

Tall, wiry Meghna with her large glasses, bigger than her eyes, but smaller than her smile that bursts across her sunlight face, rushes to greet Amma, who is right behind me.

Amma shuts the apartment door. She hugs Meghna warmly, and draws Akhila to her with a smile she had forgotten about these many years. I join the huddle. Amma mutters that she loves her daughters and one more just made us the perfect family.

The fiancé has draped herself in the sofa. I get up to return the Neelkamals, remembering a long ago Diwali night bonfire when Akhila and I burnt all of Appa's clothes swearing that no man would ever set foot inside our house again. Is that when Akhila knew?

There will be time to ask her and Meghna all that later. For now, I wonder what I will tell Meena auntie about Akhila's fiancé and her "settling down" with her girlfriend.

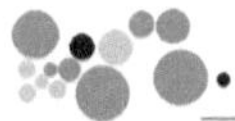

*With over twenty years of teaching experience, **Dr Preetha Vasan** currently teaches the Master's programme in English at Jyoti Nivas College, Bengaluru. A poet and author, her first publication* Yagna, *a book of poems based on* The Mahabharata, *gives voice to subalterns, while contemporising the epic through the perspective of Sanjaya.*

THE MAGGI POINT

Nasreen Khan

There it was. That little tea shack everyone had told us about. Right by the side of the river.

It was a small wooden hut, a box-like structure with a thatched roof. It had a rectangular courtyard. There were narrow wooden benches laid out around the periphery of the courtyard. Tall pine trees shaded the hut on one side. On the other side was the river. Across the river, you could see the magnificent mountains shimmering in the sun.

We were on the third day of our trek and had already walked a lot that day. Starting at dawn, we had stopped only once for a break. Walking for over six hours on an uphill, rocky path was not easy for a city dweller like me. The unusual combination of biting cold air and the clear, bright sun had made my cheeks burn. I'd feel cold with my jacket off, and I'd sweat with it on. I was uncomfortable. Once in a while I would take a sip from my water bottle, less to quench my thirst and more to lessen the load on my backpack. I was tired and longed to take a break.

I caught up with the trek leader to ask him when we would make a stop. He said it would take an hour to reach the tea shack where we could rest for half an hour. In an effort to comfort me, he said the tea seller there has the best tea I would ever have had. "You will love it," he said. "The *chai wala* has a magical knack of keeping refreshing tea and hot snacks ready to serve to trekkers as soon as they reach. I know you will enjoy his little tea shack!"

We would take a break to ready ourselves at that point, he explained. The real climb, he said, would start from there. And because the path ahead from there was narrow and risky, all ten of us would need to stay together.

The thought of resting while having hot tea and snacks was enticing! I knew that if I reached the stop before the others, I could gift myself a longer break. I sped up, leaving my group to come at their own pace.

The route to the tea shack was through a narrow path that ran alongside a river. The water gurgled and danced over the rocks along its path. On the other side of the river I could see the mountains. The glint of the sun made them seem like a mirage, appearing and disappearing at each turn I took.

It was very quiet now that I had left my group far behind. Once in a while I met local passers-by, who would guide me to the tea shack. It was reassuring to hear the sound of the river gushing by, my only companion on my journey. My legs seemed to have found a rhythm of their own, moving ahead stoically despite the ache and stiffness.

I felt like I had been walking for hours before I saw the *chai wala*.

Stooped over a dented aluminium pan kept over a coal fire, he was stoking the embers to keep them burning. His fair skin was tanned and wrinkled in the sun, a sign that he had weathered many seasons. Shining, twinkling black eyes peeped behind his now white eyelashes. He looked up to greet me with a smile as I walked towards him, his eyes revealing deep laugh lines on their edges.

A row of broken tea cups lined the shelf. He asked me what kind of tea I wanted. With ginger? With cardamom? Less sugar? With a practised hand he threw some ingredients into the pan. He asked me to make myself comfortable while he made some *pakodas* to go with the tea.

It was very quiet and peaceful there. The only sound was of the water gushing by. The air was clean and cool. I began to relax. I took my shoes off and lay down on one of the benches, looking up at the clear blue sky. I could hear the birds and crickets. The warmth of the sun and the sound of the river lulled me to sleep...

I woke with a start. A group of young trekkers had come in. They were talking in agitated voices. They all seemed to be looking at something I hadn't paid attention to. From outside the tea shack was a trail going up to the mountain that we would be climbing in a while. Some of the members of the group had gone on to explore the path. To their dismay, they discovered it was a very narrow, steep climb. In fact, some of them came and said, "The climb seems dangerous and endless – continuing as far as the eyes could see."

A young man came running to the *chai wala*. He was breathless, not so much due to the effort as the anxiety. He asked the *chai wala* if he had ever been up to the top of the mountain to see the famous glacier. The *chai wala* nodded to say he had, and without looking up, continued to stir his aluminium pan.

The young man continued, "I have been told that the glacier at the top of the mountain is very beautiful. Is it really very beautiful?" When the *chai wala* didn't answer, he continued, "I mean, look at it. It's such a tough, steep climb. There is no point going up all the way to discover it was not worth it! That's why I am asking you."

The *chai wala* didn't answer his question but looked up and asked the young man a question instead. "Which route did you take to come here? Did you cross the Maggi Point?"

The young man said, "Yes, we did."

The *chai wala* continued, "Did you stop to eat the Maggi there?"

The young man got irritated. "Yes, we did, but that was yesterday. And what does that have to do with my question?"

Unruffled, the *chai wala* asked, "How was the Maggi there? And were the pink flowers already in bloom?"

Now visibly upset, the young man replied. "It was pretty useless. The fellow there did not even cook the onions properly! And no, there were no pink flowers anywhere. There were only empty, yellow packets of Maggi lying all around creating filth! Now can you please answer my question? Is the glacier very beautiful?"

The *chai wala* shook his head. "Well, it's not as beautiful as some people claim it is. The climb is very tough and steep. So it may not be worth it for some people. But it's your choice whether you want to undertake the journey or not."

"Bah," said the man and stomped off to find his trek leader. I could hear him arguing about the plan ahead. Shortly after, I saw the group reassemble and go back the way they had come. They had decided to return. There was once again silence, broken only by the sound of the *chai wala*'s spoon stirring the brewing tea.

I settled back thoughtfully with my cup of tea, looking out for my group that I could now see coming in from a distance.

A few minutes later, I heard familiar voices. From their tone, I could sense their relief at reaching a stop. I waved to let them know I was there. As they neared, some members came into the courtyard to rest and relax. Some others went to the river to dip their tired feet in water. Still others went exploring the area. The trek leader asked us to rest well so we would be ready to climb. We needed to reach a clearing where we could pitch our tents for the night. This would take three hours of steep climbing, he said.

As he pointed at the towering mountain that we were to climb, many stunned 'aahs' could be heard. To see the full view of the mountain I had to strain my entire neck around. I felt like a tiny speck in front of it!

A few members asked the trek leader to show them the mountain trail more closely. I heard them exclaim as they went closer. One of them, whom I had become quite friendly with, came back to the courtyard. She looked at me and said, "It looks really tough. I am not sure I can make it."

She then turned to the *chai wala* and asked, "Chacha, have you ever been to that mountain top?"

He nodded his yes, without looking up. "Many times," he said.

"Is the glacier very beautiful?" she asked.

The *chai wala* gave me a knowing look. Unhurriedly, he asked my friend. "Did you stop at the Maggi Point?"

"Yes," she said. "We had our lunch there yesterday."

"Did you have Maggi there? Were the pink flowers in bloom?"

"Oh yes," she exclaimed. "The whole area was full of pink flowers. It was as if a beautiful pink carpet had been laid out in the valley."

"What about the Maggi? How was it?" he asked.

"Oh, that was delightful. I had two plates! The cook added capsicum and onion as well, so it was a wholesome, hot meal. All of us loved it!"

Turning once again to look at the towering mountain, she said, "But do tell me if you have been up this mountain. Is the glacier really very beautiful?"

The *chai wala* looked up at the mountain and nodded. "Yes," he said. "It is very beautiful. The climb is very steep and tough but the beauty you see there makes you forget how difficult it was. It is well worth the journey."

I was half-reclining and observing their conversation. On hearing this, I sat up. I was stunned. What was he saying? He had just said it was not worth it! Now he was saying it was well worth it? What was he up to?

Before I could say anything, my friend excitedly skipped out. She was keen to share this information with the others.

I gave the *chai wala* a questioning look. He met my eye but didn't say anything. I couldn't keep silent any longer, and blurted out my question. "Why did you lie to my friend?" I demanded. "She's scared of heights and if it's not worth it, she shouldn't be going!"

For a while, he didn't answer.

Then he said in a low quiet voice. "I have had this tea shop for twenty years. I have seen hundreds of people undertake this climb. And I have realised, like everything else in life, it's not about the glacier. The glacier is the same. The journey is also the same. It's about the person who sees the glacier. It's the eyes of beholder that decide its beauty."

He went on: "I always ask people the same question. Depending on their answer, I know how they look at life. So I know who will find the glacier beautiful and who will only find fault in it. The young man found only fault in the Maggi Point. He didn't even notice the pink flowers that I know are blooming throughout the valley. The young lady didn't notice the dirt of the yellow packets that I know are littered there. The view was the same. The eyes that saw it were different."

I sat in silence for a long time. I asked myself what had I noticed at the Maggi Point – did I see the flowers or did I see the filth?

He was right, life is the same. It's the eyes of beholder that decide its beauty. He had handed over the essence of life to me along with his broken tea cup.

Nasreen Khan is an executive coach, life coach, behavioural skills facilitator and NLP trainer based in Delhi. She works with individuals and organisations to support them to be their best, and brings simplicity, authenticity and commitment to whatever she chooses to do. A keen observer of human behaviour, the human mind also fascinates Nasreen. She loves travelling, being in the mountains and nature photography.

A FLIGHT TO FREEDOM

AV Sridevi

Life's dramatic changes never announce their arrival; no lightning, thunder or earth-shattering noises. Each of our stories, held in the crisscross lines of our palms, silently twist or tweak a little, even as life surprises us with its rollercoaster ride. On that particular dawn as Monica waved for a taxi and asked, "Airport?" she never thought the day was any different. The sleepy, silent roads did not whisper to her that the flight she was about to take would change her completely from within.

Monica alighted at the airport, her baby strapped safely close to her bosom. She wheeled a fluffy pink-and-white kid's bag in the shape of a bunny, perched on top of a medium-sized trolley with her right hand. Her left hand held the baby sling, as if she could trust no one but herself with the precious treasure held inside. In quick, fluid, elegant movements enhanced by the sway of her ankle-length block-printed black Jaipuri cotton skirt, she reached an IndiGo counter at the domestic terminal of Mumbai airport.

Once inside the aircraft, she laid her well-fed child on her lap and softly placed a small ball of cotton inside each of her delicate little ears. "Now!" she thought, sitting back in her window seat, "I finally have some time for myself." Monica looked out of her window, and gradually her thoughts meandered aimlessly like unruly children. Sometimes, they wandered to her waiting husband and home in Patna and suddenly out of the blue they landed up in her cousin's wedding, the reason for her week-long Mumbai trip. Unknowingly, her smile broadened as she reminisced about the fun, frolic and food of the past few days.

She now turned her head towards the aisle, a few customary, curious glances at fellow travellers in the aircraft. Her trailing thoughts screeched to a halt when she saw a face from her past entering the aircraft. She froze in cold sweat. For years she had formed words, erased them, and reworded what she would say if she ever met this person. Involuntarily, she started chanting the Gayatri Mantra under her breath, the way she did whenever she needed solace and succour.

As the figure advanced into the aircraft, searching for her seat, the first thought that came to Monica's mind was how kind time had been in preserving her once-best-friend's charming looks. But for a few faint lines on her face, which only added dignity, Sneha looked the way she had some fifteen years ago. Monica thanked her stars for the soundly sleeping baby on her lap and a rescue in her window seat. Though she glued her eyes to the glass, she could hardly register anything of the happenings outside. Her sensory faculties were heightened as she waited for Sneha to walk past to her own seat, as far away from Monica's as possible.

In the next few tormenting moments, Monica's heart began thumping wild drumbeats within her when she heard the rustling of fabric and footsteps near her own seat. Then, an unmistakable gasp from the person looking for her seat. From Sneha. Though Monica continued to look out of the window, she made a mental note of her companion's movements, of her shoving hand luggage into the overhead compartment, the buckling of the seat belt and then Sneha's reluctant settling down. Next to her.

The plane began racing on the tarmac and Monica's thoughts raced backwards into the past, with equal speed. She could see herself and Sneha, a decade and half younger from now, entering their college gates in pleated skirts and ponytails. It seemed like just yesterday that they were having this conversation.

"Monica, promise me you won't tell this to anyone? Not even to my mother? I just scraped through the trigonometry class test we had yesterday. First time for me. I have to spend more time in the company of mathematics and less in yours," Sneha said, dismally.

Monica replied, "Sneha, I promise I won't feel bad. In return, you must not go complaining to my mother that I give you my lunchbox and eat yours instead. I must say, your mother has magic in her hands."

Both friends shared myriad childhood memories, secrets and giggles familiar only to carefree youth, and were inseparable throughout the day. All the contents of their teenage hearts were poured into each other's ears. Well, almost all. Monica, of late was troubled by a hazy cloud of jealousy that suddenly popped up within her.

Especially on days when Roshan, the new boy in their class, started looking obliquely at Sneha with his feelings written on his face. On those days, Monica found something burning within her.

It was she who had a crush on Roshan and not Sneha, thought Monica with a fierce feeling of possessiveness. One lucky day, when Providence offered a chance, Monica readily grabbed it. She overheard him say to someone in their biology practical group that he found drawing quite tedious. How could she not try to gain his attention? She offered a helping hand and spent an entire night working hard to make each drawing look neat and perfect. The next day, when she handed his completed book back to him, Roshan thanked her profusely. As he walked beside her handing over a big blue packet of Cadbury Dairy Milk, he said affectionately, "Monica, I know that buying this for you is nowhere comparable to the efforts and time you have put in for me. Thank you so much, it was really sweet of you and a big relief for a pathetic artist like me."

Monica was on cloud nine walking with Roshan, imagining coffee dates, movies... and then suddenly Roshan's words brought her back to cruel reality.

"Monica, will you please give this to your best friend Sneha?" Roshan handed over one more chocolate bar, blushing deep red as he uttered Sneha's name.

As the weeks progressed, the brown chocolate graduated to flowers of various colours and then to red roses. Now, Sneha and Roshan didn't even need Monica to mediate. The tiny ball of jealousy in Monica's heart assumed giant proportions, consuming all the space.

Gradually, the green monster devoured all the love and friendship that had been reserved for Sneha. All that remained behind in its place was an adamant, persistent demand for Roshan's attention. Monica decided she would have it. By hook or by crook.

Monica remembered a long-gone winter night when she was a child, tucked inside her blanket. Her parents thought that she was sleeping. Her sleepy eyes opened wide inside the blanket when she heard them speaking in furtive whispers about Sneha's adoption when Sneha was a seven-month-old baby. Sleep came quite late to her that night. Suddenly, she remembered those whispers now. On the pretext of delivering a secret letter from Sneha, Monica fixed up a meeting with Roshan who came like an eager lover, but left with a befuddled heart. Instead of the promised letter, all Roshan got was advice to stay away from Sneha. Monica asked him, "She doesn't even know her past, her parents, Roshan, and how can you think of your future with her?" Monica felt both hopeful and burdened as she blurted out these words. Hopeful, that Roshan may choose her instead of Sneha. Burdened, as she knew she could never forgive herself for betraying her closest friend. All the vexing vagaries of a young heart tormented her, making her miserable.

A few days after Monica's surreptitious meeting with Roshan, Sneha entered her best friend's house like a storm. She raved and ranted, her face turning crimson with rage. Monica grew crestfallen as she realised through Sneha's outpourings that Roshan continued to pledge his love and support to Sneha. The guilt in Monica's heart weighed so much on her mouth that no word could escape; they simply flowed down her eyes as copious tears. But Sneha did not stay back to wipe them. In fact, she never looked back once in all these years. Monica was too ashamed of herself to summon up the courage to visit Sneha's house to ask for forgiveness. That was the last time the friends met face-to-face. Until now.

A sudden turbulence jolted Monica to the present. She rocked her disturbed infant back to sleep and turned to face her silent companion who was sitting stoically, gazing at the in-flight magazine. A little hesitantly, she said, "Hi Sneha, I am Monica. I hope you remember me?" She regretted her opening words as soon as they were out, wishing she could have said something better. Her companion lifted her steady gaze and replied with unsubtle sarcasm, "Monica, how can I forget you?"

And then, suddenly, somewhere from the limitless skies around, Monica found the courage to unlock her feelings and words. They simply flowed from her heart, "Sneha, I know I am fifteen years late in asking, but will you please forgive me? I know I should not have been, but I was so jealous of you. You can never imagine how that one folly of mine placed a boulder of burden that I have been carrying within me ever since that ill-fated evening."

Sneha looked at her rigidly and replied drily, "It is alright. I have nothing else to say nor do I want to hear about it."

Monica continued, as if the flood of feelings had broken a barrage that could not be controlled, "For years, my husband and I tried having a baby, but fate had something else in store for us. We depended on science, faith and nature, but when all of them failed we decided to adopt a child." Introducing the sleeping child on her lap, Monica said, "She is Sneha, your namesake." With this unexpected revelation Sneha was visibly shaken, but Monica continued, her voice now quivering with emotion as she admitted the guilt and grief she had suppressed all this time, "I think it was destiny's way of showing me my redemption."

Sneha was moved beyond words. She was unprepared to hear about this torture her friend had undergone. Her gentle nature easily melted her hardened demeanour towards Monica. Softly, she held her friend's hand and said, "Monica, I am deeply touched about your naming your baby after me. Please don't feel bad any further, the past is over and well behind us. Let it not bother you anymore."

Sneha continued, "In hindsight, I think you did more good than harm to me. Your disclosure of my secret saved me a great deal of trouble of when and how to put it across to Roshan. I was always so unsure of how he and his family would react to the news of my adoption. It also proved Roshan's strength of character and his support for me. At times, I wonder if you had unknowingly made things easier for me. Honestly, though, at that time, anger wrapped my eyes tightly, making me blind to all the positive outcomes and only magnified your treachery. But today, much wiser after life's lessons, I would rather blame it on our turbulent age – we were both so foolishly young then." Monica was astounded to hear Sneha's confession.

The flight landed and both friends parted at Patna airport to their respective lives, but not before they embraced each other, exchanged numbers, addresses and hurriedly bridged the gap of all those lost years. As Monica stepped out of the airport holding her luggage and her little Sneha, she realised she had not felt this lighthearted in ages. The guilt trapped within her for years was left behind in the flight. Today, finally, she felt free.

AV Sridevi is an MBA by qualification and a homemaker by choice. A passionate reader, her love for words took a new turn when she held her pen and gave flight to her imagination. She currently lives in Mumbai with her husband and two sons.

NAVJOTE NU BHONU (THE NAVJOTE FEAST)

Sulekha Bajpai

Danish Wadia woke up with a start. How could he have slept in so late? The sun had been streaming into the neatly arranged room through the faded, nylon curtains. The warmth of the sunrays on his body felt like Mama waking him up like she used to. Now, there was no Mama, no family, no home and, alas, no hot meals either. In this clinically clean room, the only sign of her presence was her old birthday sari that Danish had recycled as curtains for his window. Mama had left him no money at all but she had left him this one room and a cranky landlord. Danish had inherited the tenancy and though the landlord hated his face, he couldn't evict him.

Danish meticulously folded each day's newspaper and arranged it into a neat pile. At ₹10 a kg, the *raddi* fetched him a good ₹60 every two weeks. It was good enough to buy plantains for breakfast. He had one every morning with a cup of toned milk. The milk came free from renting out the porch for the milkman to sleep at night. Cousins from Calcutta sent him Darjeeling tea on and off. He didn't care much for Darjeeling tea but he had it every morning because he didn't have to pay for it. He used honey in his tea for two reasons: to keep him trim; it was collected from the rain tree that Mama had planted thirty years ago. The boys gave him five kilos of it and he let them sell the rest in the neighborhood. Come to think of it, what would he have done without Mama's care for him even after she left? He was well-aware but continued to do nothing with himself.

If Mama were alive today, she would be 82 years old and probably the world's biggest nag. Naturally, what caring mother wouldn't have nagged a wastrel of a son such as him? Her love for him had nothing to do with him. She loved him in spite of who he was. If she were here, she would have never let him stay a bachelor so long, pushing 43. How time flies!

It was already lunchtime with Danish just finishing his bath, shave, breakfast and paper. There was some meat in the freezer to be had with last night's chapattis. The best thing about Jerbano's dinner-*dabba* was that it saw him through next day's lunch. While the meat thawed, he polished Dad's old pair of Italian shoes. Wasn't it the pair that Dad purchased with Shireen aunty's birthday money for him? It was rather mean of him to buy a present for himself with it. It didn't matter now. The pair looked just right with Dad's grey suit that he was wearing to the evening's Navjote ceremony. What luck that he had spotted the news item in *Mumbai Times*! Who says there's nothing like a free lunch? Here was a free dinner and what a feast it promised to be.

All suited and booted, Danish felt he had now earned his dinner by walking four kilometers to reach Cama Baug, the venue of the Navjote. Just as he approached the decorated garden gate, he noticed a taxi stopped outside. A young mother was struggling to retrieve her sleeping child from the back seat. Danish offered to help immediately not because he couldn't bear to see her pencil-heel crack under the child's weight but simply because carrying a sleeping child could well become his passport. "Excuse me, Ma'am, *hun tamune help karu ke*? (Can I help?)" and he carried the child before she could react. They walked in as a couple without anyone suspecting him.

The incense, the divas, and the tuberoses had created a heady scent that hit Danish so suddenly that he wanted to cry. He reminisced about his own Navjote ceremony. All the fuss that his whole family had put him through! Sweaty aunts kissing his soft nine-year-old face and those horrible lipstick marks on his white *dagli*. How they had smothered him then with affection and now he longed for a familiar smile. Suddenly, a waiter interrupted his reverie. "Sir, Coke for you?" Danish gulped it down in one breath. He felt braced for the evening and he gravitated towards the bar to opt for a rum and Coke. There was only so much time to drink before dinner.

With his drink in hand, he looked for a safe seat. He found a group of quaint old ladies all aged 82 and upwards. It wasn't difficult to converse with them. All you had to do was smile and exclaim, "*Dinoo ketli saras lagi ni? Backless choli ma tim taraak!* (Dinoo looks lovely in a backless blouse!)" They would laugh loudly and go off on a tangent. Danish excused himself to refill his glass and now selected another lady with a hearing aid. The wait for the dinner became a trifle easier. She would say something and he would smile and nod, never making the mistake of saying anything to trigger conversation. Mentally, he was weighing the pros and cons of trying a Campari.

Danish was about to move away from the oldie club but he froze in his tracks. She was the most stunning woman he had seen in years. She was blissfully unaware of the milieu sipping quietly on her drink. Dressed in a subtle brocade sari, the baby-pink truly became her. Simple, matte-gold jewellery, her glistening white teeth, and an abruptly short haircut set her apart from the other matronly looking women. Danish wanted to leap across and catch her attention with something as inane as, "Do I know you from somewhere?" He was straining at the leash to say something to her but he allowed the momentary urge to pass like always. He just smiled to himself without the world knowing.

The stunning woman that Danish had eyes for knocked the cobalt blue drink on to her lovely sari, all because a silly child didn't see where he was going. Danish leapt at her with a napkin. Before she could register the fuss, he had produced more napkins from nearby tables and salvaged her sari.

Surprisingly, she was unflustered and thanked him immensely. "Hi, I'm Mehnaaz Barucha," she said in a husky voice. Danish felt something crawl at his earlobe like it always did when he was secretly pleased. The Navjote ceremony was continuing in the background and the bulk of the guests had moved there. Some nostalgic Bawa had replaced the new-age music with some old love song. She asked him where he worked. "I do voluntary work for Dilkhush School. *Mane charity nu kaam game che* (I like working for charities)," he said. "I'm a journalist," Mehnaaz said smiling at him. He felt compelled to ask her for a dance. She blushed a little and then allowed herself to be led by him. They looked handsome together. Danish was desperately trying to cover up his shyness by making conversation. "*Tamaro journalism nu job bahu interesting che, ni*? (Isn't journalism an interesting job?)" She said she loved writing and getting paid well for something she loved. The magic was positively growing and Danish was the passive recipient, not its creator.

The incense and the marigolds, the tuberoses and the lilies now had to struggle with another competing aroma. Danish's eyes darted to the seating area already looking for the best spot for them. Maybe a convenient corner seat that would allow a swift escape, in case some familiar nerd insisted on joining him for dinner. He still couldn't handle the fear of getting caught in the act. Mehnaaz got the corner seats. The freshly washed banana leaf titillated him. The *achar*, the *rotli*, the *sariyas* and the wafers had already started the countdown in his starved head. One by one, the delicacies began showing up on the green leaf. The finely browned frill cutlets had a very crispy exterior. They always rolled it on a bed of *rava* to give it that crunch that he so loved to bite into. Thank god it wasn't *saas ni macchi* being served but his favourite *patra ni macchi* that was making the rounds. Danish decided that the *patra ni macchi* could definitely never taste like the one Mama and Katy Maasi cooked together at his home over cups of coffee and dollops of gossip.

Danish ate hungrily, oblivious to the surroundings until he heard a faint voice from another planet offering him a cold drink. It was Mehnaaz. Danish noticed she was eating patiently and peacefully. Danish dabbed his brow with a kerchief more out of embarrassment than perspiration. He was attacking the meat *pulao* when he noticed the hostess smile at them. She was exuberant with her "*Jamjo ji*". Danish decided to not entertain her lest she come up to them. But without looking up, he could sense her walking in their direction. Food stuffed in his mouth, he was speechless. The brain signals seemed feeble and reluctant to register her. There was no escape route. Suddenly, he heard Mehnaaz say, "Hello Aunty, how are you?" The hostess beamed at her saying, "I am fine, *dikra. Am kem? Kai khatyu nathi? Thodo topli paneer le ni?* (Some more *topli paneer* for you, dear?") She got the waiter to serve them some more. She smiled at Danish. The gold cap on her tooth flashed irritatingly and a tad threateningly. How he hoped the huge floor fan hadn't been placed so close to his chair. This silly fan was responsible for attracting the 'gold-toothed monster' to them.

What he dreaded most was beckoning and he couldn't do a thing about it. The monster smiled at Mehnaaz and said, "Dear, your name was...?" Mehnaaz smiled a reassuring and confident smile and said promptly, "I'm Behroze Banker. I teach at Cyrus's School. Higher level English at St. Mary's." "Oh, yes of course! How silly of me, dear!" Just then the monster's husband whisked her away to introduce her to some other guests. Danish was dumbfounded. Was it that he had had too much to drink? He always believed that faith could move mountains but didn't know that food could metamorphose people.

Mehnaaz Bharucha, the journalist had just turned into Behroze Banker, the English teacher. Food indeed possessed the power to change people. Had it not driven him from being Mama's Dinoo to Danish Wadia, the freeloader?

The air was filled with cheers but Danish's gaze refused to move. It was fixed on Mehnaaz, Behroze or whoever she was. His jaw was locked. Her confident gaze unlocked it. He stumbled and settled for "St. Mary's School?" With a charming tilt to her head, she said effortlessly, "That's the school Cyrus studies at." "Cyrus?" he asked, opening and closing his mouth like a goldfish. "That's the kid whose Navjote you are at tonight, my dear!"

Danish came to ground reality after having travelled to another planet with the 'Bhonu'. Someone had taken the wind out of his sails. She continued to sail with the tide. With a flourish, she opened her purse, stopped and gave him a look that threw one more challenge at him. She gently placed a newspaper cutting circled in red on the table. "*Lagan nu bhonu khase? Mari sathe awse kaale chha vage?* (Care for a wedding feast? Join me tomorrow at six p.m.?)"

The colour slowly returned to his face, the voice showed no signs. He continued to look at her with an expressionless, childlike stare. She added nonchalantly, "Don't you forget to do your homework this time, and thoroughly!"

He felt like a pair of strong wings had been spread out. He felt himself moving safely under them. This was the first time after Mama that he felt sheltered. Safe, once again.

Sulekha Bajpai *is a bi-lingual script, story, dialogue and lyrics writer, a published poet as well as an advertising professional based in Mumbai. Her creativity is fuelled by her love for travelling and interacting with new cultures, as well as a keen appreciation of authenticity and realism in human interactions.*

A PROMISE IS A PROMISE

Natasha Sharma

The car backfired; I was startled out of my ennui. Sleepy, jittery the entire morning, and the lecture wasn't helping either. The history class yawned its way to the half-hour mark; I had to literally hold my eyes apart. "I must stop the late-night Netflix streaming. I promised ma this morning, no more sleeping late, I'm sleeping on time, getting up fresh, so the history teacher can't put me into slumberland, again. It's going to be tough to keep my *no-more-Netflix* vow to her, but a promise is a promise," I repeated, as a mantra. The backfiring car did the trick; I was wide-awake, and actually alert. The rest of the class was lost in the perils of World War II and Hitler's rise. Since I joined the party late, I had no interest – either in Hitler or his peccadilloes. "I'd die for a coffee, though," I thought as I stifled a yawn threatening to divide my face into two halves, forever. The car, bless its weak engine, backfired again, the noise appearing somewhat closer, accompanied by some other sounds. The history teacher droned on about the fall of the Third Reich, while I fantasised about the bell ringing, ending the verbal torture. Suddenly, there was a whizz of excitement tinged with trepidation in the room – Ms Morris had announced a surprise test! Most of the class grumbled, but she stood firm. Wielding the test papers like a sword, she shushed us all.

"Thirty minutes, thirty marks. The test covers the last class, where we studied how the United States was dragged into World War II, after the Pearl Harbour attacks. Don't worry, this time the test is fairly straightforward – and simple," she grinned, dramatically.

More grumbling ensued. Ms Morris's 'simple papers' were legendary, her standard of simplicity didn't agree with that of the general public. Silence reigned after the flurry of paper-passing, while the class scratched its collective head over the conundrums thought up by Ms Morris. Five minutes of test solving had elapsed when the errant car backfired again, accompanied by other disturbing sounds. The silence in the room accentuated the ominous noise from outside. All students looked up as running footsteps beat a tattoo against the floor, somewhere at the start of the corridor. Our class was the last one in the long passage of classes, the corner one.

"Students, please ignore the noises outside. I'm not marking you on your reactivity to them, rather on your assessment of the Allied Forces. Please continue working on your test paper. It sounds like we're under attack from the Germans!" Ms Morris joked.

Most heads went back to wrestling with the questions; mine was the sole one to stay up. Except with divine intervention, I had no hopes of clearing the test. I could ace the paper if it were on Korean sitcoms; history, not so much.

"Maybe they should make a web series on World War II, then I'll be able to pass with flying colours," I thought morosely to myself, finally looking down at my pristine, white and very blank answer sheet.

The running feet sounded closer this time, prompting Ms Morris to finally rise with exasperation to investigate, and possibly admonish the culprit. She moved her massive girth to the closed door, opening it and looking out. Her partial egress ended in a collision with the teacher of the opposite room. They both exchanged clueless looks. Just then, Ms Morris decided the event needed further scrutiny.

After giving us the death glare, she stepped into the corridor. "And, what do you think you are doing, mister..." her voice was cut short, followed by a loud staccato sound, and her cry of pain.

The class sat up in surprise and fear. Most of them sprinted to the open door to peek out. We saw Ms Morris on the floor, near the start of the corridor, bleeding profusely. She was breathing heavily, her eyes were open, and blood was flowing from her mouth. Sara rushed to her side, taking her head in her lap, bending down to whisper something into Ms Morris ears. The moment was shattered by the shooter, who was brandishing a black semi-automatic machine gun with an enormous ammunition belt running across his chest. He took aim at the shrinking Sara and pelted her with bullets. Sara screamed and fell over Ms Morris. There was pandemonium in the classes, some students came out of their rooms, and were met with bullets. The shooter, a boy I vaguely recognised, began shooting indiscriminately, not caring whom he hit – or missed. People started falling all around us, I could see rows of people – teachers, students who lay on the floor, in various stages of dying. The boy's eyes were dead, there were tear streaks on his cheeks. He wiped his flowing nose with the back of his hand, the same hand that held the gun. He yelled something; the words escaped me as he started to negotiate the path, strewn with slain bodies, towards the end of the corridor. This propelled most of us to action, we ran inside our class and closed the door, moving heavy benches against it as additional backup. We could hear the sound of gunfire outside, mixed with howls of pain and sobbing. We started crying, each one of us, as we crouched against the wall. Some started praying, some writing notes to their loved ones. I was in shock, tears running down my cheeks as I heard my fellow students lay their lives down for a purpose I couldn't understand, wondering if – or maybe when – I would be next.

The shooting stopped for a while. The silence around us broken only by occasional grunts or cries of pain. It was punctured by the siren – the police were coming! We heard the shooter – I could finally place him as the weird boy in Math – yell something again, and the nonstop firing resumed. We could hear him pushing against the door of our class, prompting more tears, and more furious prayers. The door crashed, and the screaming and firing picked up again. The proximity of both was shattering, and the fear was overpowering. We crouched under the remaining benches, pushed against the wall, and decided against the futility of escaping. The shooter was in the classroom, cursing and shooting, and maybe crying. We could hear sobs tear themselves out of him as he pulled the trigger, wiping the lives of so many, in one swoop. The police had reached the school; the sirens could be heard right outside our window. We could hear the police running along the hallway, and then stopping, screaming for his surrender.

The arrival of the police officers ignited within us a flicker of hope, and this tiny iota of hope sprung my thoughts to life. I didn't want to die – and die at the hands of a boy I barely knew. I had so many dreams, so many things to do, so many times to fall before I could rise, so many books to read, so many bridges to cross. I thought of my mother, and all I wanted – now, more than ever – was to be in her arms, in her warm embrace. Her hair tickling my nose as I leaned against her, safe, protected. I wanted to feel her kiss on my forehead, like I did this morning. I wanted to feel her words against my ear, saying she loved me. I wanted to feel her breath when she leaned in, tightening the hug, crushing me against her. I wanted to eat the hot *aloo parathas*, with extra butter, she made every Friday night! I wanted my mother, I wanted her to save me from this nightmare – this sobbing, crazy shooter. I didn't want to die. I didn't want to be erased from the world without first making my mark, and I wanted to see my mother again.

Outside the window, we could hear cars drive in. The parents who had heard the news were beginning to congregate at the school, I could hear some crying. I wondered if my mother was outside, frantically looking for me. Tears ran down my face, my sobs catching in my throat. She could be so close and yet a simple wall separated us – like a line between life and death. Between the living and the dying. A prayer escaped me. I could see the test papers flutter in the air, before gracefully landing on the floor, and I realised it wasn't the car backfiring, but the sound of the gun emptying its magazine all this while. I shook my head at my stupidity. I could hear the police talking to the shooter using the school communicator, and his muffled responses. Then a thud! He was at our class door, banging at it, straining against the benches we had piled. He shot at the door, a couple of times. The cacophony of wailing outside, coupled with the screaming and crying inside, deafened me. He shot at the door again, damaging the lock. The only things stopping him were the benches. He rammed himself against the door. The officers' voices sounded closer. The door gave way as the shooter barged into our class, amidst the screaming, his machine gun cocked and ready to fire.

***

The police eventually managed to shoot him down, much as he had shot the others, experiencing a shared fate. Anxious parents waited outside the high school – for the news of their children, their hearts beating furiously. It was total chaos, with parents pushing against the police line, and ambulance and paramedics everywhere. Bodies wrapped in body bags could be seen, being carried on the gurneys. Emergency medical technicians were attending to the dying, and some to the living, who had fainted on seeing their loved ones. My mother stood by the side, harassing a young policeman, "Sir, have you seen my daughter, her class was the last one in the corridor. Sir, can you please answer me? Have you seen my daughter? This is her photograph." The novice police officer took the photograph and looked at it, not really seeing it, "I'll look around ma'am. Some of the survivors are with the paramedics, they are checking them out. Let me go and check," he said, making his escape under my mother's watchful, teary eyes.

My mother looked around with growing despair as emotional parents hugged their weeping offspring, while her arms remained – achingly – empty. Life changed for her in that moment, as it did for me. Only in my case, mine wasn't living anymore, and hers, an endless, peerless abyss of pain. Many lives were changed and snuffed out that day, one deserved and others innocent, blameless. My mother's eyes searched for me, hope against hope – for me to rush into her arms. For me to feel her kiss on my forehead. For me to feel her words against my ear, saying she loved me. For her to protect me in her arms, save me. But my words were silent, my voice unheard. I couldn't wipe the single tear that coursed down her left cheek, her eyes, now empty. I couldn't hold her as she fell on the floor, broken. You see, I couldn't unzip the black body bag I was sheathed in. I couldn't say my last goodbye, or blow my last kiss. The only thing I could do – and did – was honour the promise I made to my mother this morning, I'd stop watching Netflix. I kept my promise, ma.

Natasha Sharma is a software developer based in Pune. A "Navy brat" whose father fought in the 1971 Indo-Pak war, she spends each day arguing with her eight-going-on-sixteen daughter, and taking long walks with her dog Biscuit. Writing was always on the cards, and in the past year, she has dabbled in short stories and poetry.

LA BELLA REVENGA

Shalini Mullick

The app showed no cabs, not even with a surge fee. That was all she needed, after the terrible day. She could cry. Then salt tingled on her lips despite the pouring rain, and she realised she was already crying.

She clicked on the 'share ride' tab, one she usually avoided. Nothing usual about today anyway, she sighed, and booked the solitary one that was moving in her direction.

The five-minute wait seemed like a five-hour long movie reel of flashbacks from her relationship with Tarun. The supportive significant other, the whirlwind romance, the loving business partner – everything had been a façade. The reality was stark and ugly, and still unfathomable for the most part.

"Yes, the account is empty, Aditi."

She had stared at him, unable to get a word out.

"But we need to pay off the loans, and plan the wedding too!"

"Aditi, you are so naïve. There is no money. There is no wedding either. The loan is your problem."

Just like that, life had turned upside down.

Tarun had led her on, taken advantage of her and their purported relationship to siphon off the profits from her new venture. She had taken a loan for her startup, and alienated her parents because they didn't approve of her relationship with Tarun. The affair had been a ruse she had fallen for, and he had betrayed her trust both emotionally and financially.

It was all over. He had left her hurt, heartbroken and broke.

He was right. She was naïve.

She had been a fool to ignore all those red flags.

The reluctance to share the accounts with her, his handling all the meeting with the bankers, the hushed conversations on his phone, the need for secrecy, the excuses for not showing up... It all added up.

Some more tears later, the cab drew up.

Once inside, glad for the shelter, she used her stole to wipe her dripping wet hair and face.

"Madam, location correct *hai na*? (Is the location correct?)"

"*Haan* (yes)."

The cab began to slowly weave its way out of the chaotic traffic. The driver was as disinterested in her as her co-passenger, a lady close to her own age. That was a relief. The last thing she needed was a bunch of nosy co-passengers in a packed share ride, or to get her wet tote bag on someone else's elbows. The other woman's phone rang.

"The job is done? Are you sure? You have pictures?"

She couldn't hear what the person on the other side was saying, but saw the woman's face contort as she tried to control her tears.

"I want you to hand over the complete package to me the next time we meet. All pictures of them together, copies of hotel bills, flight tickets, everything."

The woman hung up and slammed the phone on the seat between them. She looked out of her window, but Aditi could sense her suppressing the sobs racking her body. After a few minutes of trying to compose herself, the lady reached for her handbag.

The vehicle swerved, even as the lady was busy rummaging in her bag for something.

The phone dropped to the floor and Aditi bent down to pick it up.

A pair of soft brown eyes stared back at her.

She was taken aback.

That picture, those eyes… so familiar.

Surely, this was a mistake.

After all, she had never seen the pup in question before, just seen pictures. Like this one.

She gingerly replaced the phone back on the seat.

Immediately, the lady grabbed it and dialed a number from a card she had pulled out of her bag.

"Get the papers ready. But keep it confidential. I don't want him to get even a whiff of all this. He will pay dearly. The proof given by the detective will be sent with the notice so he can't hedge his way out of this. I will destroy him."

Her controlled tone was in contrast to the tears flowing down her cheeks when she hung up and put the phone back on the seat.

Aditi used the woman's distraction to study her phone's wallpaper picture carefully.

It wasn't just the pup. It was the backdrop.

The pup in its red cushioned bed, the decor in the background.

No doubt about it. Same picture.

Could this be true? Was this what it seemed to be?

"Why would I marry you? I was just using you to get out of a financial mess, Aditi. I am happily married. I have a home, a family with my pooch, and a rocking social life. Why would I disturb that? You were the one who kept talking about a wedding, not me."

Everyone called her impulsive. But she had always been a fast-thinker. That's how she had worked through client meetings, got contracts and made profits before people expected her to.

Profits that Tarun had siphoned, leaving her behind schedule in her payments and in debt.

Shocked and hurt she certainly was, but she was still the same Aditi who could think on her feet. Even in this shared cab with a co-passenger who had to be Tarun's wife.

The wife he went back to every day; the wife he had left her for after their three-year relationship.

Also, the wife who had hired detectives and lawyers and would be sending him a divorce notice shortly.

Aditi broke the ice with her co-passenger.

"Aditi," she introduced herself.

"Gauri."

"Lovely dog," Aditi indicated the wallpaper. "Is it a Lhasa Apso?'

"Oh, no! This is a Shih Tzu."

"Oh! I don't know much about dogs. My kid sister loves them and keeps asking for one as a pet."

"You should get one. They are loyal and loving."

"Hmm. I don't know. Seems like a good idea. But looking after them is an effort. Does everyone at home pitch in with him?"

"Her. Her name is Bella. Yes, my husband and I look after her together. He loves her a lot."

Even though she had been sure that the picture was the same, hearing Bella's name spoken aloud startled Aditi. She had heard so much from Tarun about his dear pet. She fought her emotions to keep the conversation going.

"That's great. You make a lovely family."

"Yes, a family that will soon be a broken family."

Aditi pretended she hadn't heard and waited for Gauri to continue. This was her chance.

She was disappointed.

Gauri changed the topic.

"It has been raining so heavily the past week."

"Yes." Aditi realised Gauri wouldn't speak about her family again. "So, are you going to MG road?"

"Yes, I am meeting some friends there for coffee. What about you?"

Aditi had been headed home so she could bury her head in her comforter and cry her heart out.

That could wait.

"I am also meeting some friends. Actually, if you don't mind, I wanted to ask you something," Aditi said.

"What?"

"My friends and I took the 'selfie-with-a-new-friend' challenge on Facebook, where we post selfies with new friends and tag them. I am headed to meet these girls. Unfortunately, I have had a busy week, and I am short of selfies. Could we have a selfie together? Hopefully, it will help me match the count of my friends!"

Gauri smiled. "Sure."

She fished out a small mirror from her bag and refreshed her lipstick.

Aditi draped her stole with a fashionable knot.

They came closer to each other and smiled as Aditi held out her phone camera and clicked away.

"Nice!" Gauri looked at the picture that showed her smiling, her hair falling across her face.

"I will send you the pictures. And send you a Facebook request too."

They exchanged numbers.

The cab pulled up at Café Italiano on MG Road. Gauri picked up her phone to pay for the cab ride, and waved to Aditi. "Bye, all the best for your challenge!"

Aditi smiled. She believed she had aced this challenge.

A few more minutes and she would be home.

She knew what she wanted, and like always, she would get it.

Revenge is a dish that is best had cold, but she fixed herself a large steaming coffee before composing the message.

"Tarun, you are right. There will be no marriage. And not just with me. If you don't repay the money that you have stolen from me within three days, I will expose you to your wife."

She pressed send. Once the two blue ticks appeared on her screen, she returned to the coffee.

She finished the coffee at a leisurely pace, enjoying the froth of the cappuccino. She knew Tarun would have typed his reply, with a vengeance, and would be waiting to carry the chat forward. Well, he could wait.

"You are bluffing. How can you expose me? You didn't even know that I was married till a few hours ago. Aditi, I am not a fool like you. I have been very careful. You won't even be able to find me once I change my mobile number."

"Yes, Tarun. A lot changes in a few hours. Today morning I was dreaming of our wedding. Now, I am speaking of ending your marriage. And it is Gauri I will need to find, not you."

The tick marks did turn blue, but Tarun was too dumbstruck to type back.

"Yes. Gauri. Your wife. I know her name. I know her too."

I also know she will divorce you soon. And I must act before that, Aditi thought, and pressed 'send'.

"Aditi, understand. Things change. Relationships change."

He was flabbergasted.

"Life also changes, Tarun. Mine did. Yours is about to."

Even a shared cab ride can be a life-changing experience, she thought.

And with that she sent Tarun the picture.

Aditi and Gauri, smiling; their arms across the other's shoulders, pouting, on the backseat of a sedan. Two girlfriends, looking fresh and ready for an evening out.

She fell asleep even before she could check the read receipts. It had been a really long day after all.

The next day, her SMS beeped. "Your account 456xxxxxx9865 is credited by INR 5,00,000."

She smiled.

The surprises were just beginning for Tarun.

The divorce notice he would receive soon would be the perfect top-up for the selfie of Aditi and Gauri smiling together.

The cab ride he hadn't even taken had changed his life completely, hadn't it?

Dr Shalini Mullick is a keen reader-turned-writer, who writes nonfiction, poetry and fiction. She is also a practising doctor, specialising in pulmonary pathology. Her short stories and flash-fiction contributions are regularly featured on online platforms and have been published in anthologies.

THE CAR KEYS

Noopur Joshi Bapat

Sudha could hear voices, a rather heated argument, from the next room. It was Shashank and Rashi's bedroom, her son and daughter-in-law. She had sensed something amiss between the two of them since morning; she knew this was coming. She hurried towards the living room and came back even quicker. Her job was done.

"Damn, where are the car keys?" Shashank was irritated. Sudha saw her son rush out of the bedroom and search frantically for his car keys. She tightened her fist. It was only after Shashank went back to his room in defeat that she heaved a sigh of relief.

The next morning, she woke up to cheerful banter across the living room; Shikhar, her grandson, was getting ready for school and Rashi and Shashank were helping him out, occasionally passing each other glances of affection. The storm had passed.

"Ma, we are leaving for work. Rashi, did you see the car ke... oh, they are right here. I couldn't find them here last night."

"Anger blurs your mind and vision, you tend not to see things right in front of you, Shashank." Sudha placed her hand on her son's head. "Rashi, please get me my medicines while coming back, these will only last for a couple of days more."

"Sure, Ma, I'll take your prescription," Rashi said.

Sudha waved them goodbye and kept watching till the car was out of sight.

**

"Poonam, you go ahead and clean up the house, I am resting in my room." Leaving instructions for her domestic helper, Sudha retired to her bedroom, securely closing the door behind her. She opened her wardrobe and pulled out a photo album kept beneath her neatly stacked saris.

Caressing the pictures, she remembered the happy times, her little world. Sudhir, her loving husband and a doting father to Shashank. His only shortcoming was his impulsiveness and short temper. Shashank was exactly like his father. Sudha's forehead puckered.

Sudha placed back the photo album back neatly and closed the wardrobe.

**

"Shashank, can you take a cab today to office? I need to go to Shikhar's school for the parent-teacher meeting today," Rashi said to her husband as she collected her bag and belongings. "I will pick you up in the evening. Where are the car keys?"

"Mumma, how come every time we go to school for the PTM, you cannot find the car keys?" Shikhar complained, his eyes glued to the game he was playing on his mobile phone.

"Let me book a cab quickly, looking for the keys will kill more time."

A couple of hours later, Rashi and Shikhar returned home, Rashi rather furious and Shikhar almost sobbing.

"Shikhar, go to your room immediately and start studying. And don't you dare come out till lunch. Ma, can you please keep an eye on him so that he doesn't sneak out to watch TV?"

"Don't worry, Rashi, he is just a child, he will take things seriously once he is a bit older. Remember, childhood comes only once, and it is not supposed to be spent in locked rooms. I will make sure he studies well but will give him some free time to go out and play. Don't worry. You go to work," Sudha reassured her and patted her cheek lovingly.

"I tried to reason with her, Ma, but she won't listen." Shashank chuckled. "She is one paranoid mother."

"Let me book another cab," Rashi said, distractedly.

"The keys are right here, we can go by car," Shashank said, pulling the keys from the key holder in the living room.

"They were not here when I looked in the morning."

"Anger blurs your mind and vision, you tend not to see things right in front of you," Sudha remarked, walking towards the kitchen.

**

Later that night, Sudha overheard Rashi and Shashank talking.

"Shashank, it was quite strange today. While leaving for school, I could not find the car keys, but you found them exactly where they're always kept. There is something fishy."

"It has always been that way Rashi, as long as I remember. And it is not for this particular car, either. It's happened for all the cars that we owned all these years; the keys disappear and after a while are magically found in their original place."

"So this would happen even when your dad was there?"

"I was too young to remember, but ever since I started driving, it has been this way."

"I don't mean to sound suspicious, but have you ever thought of asking Ma about this?"

"I had given it a thought, but it didn't make sense. Why would she take the keys? And even if she did, why would she put them back later?"

"That's true, but..."

"Every house has its secrets, this is ours," Shashank said slyly.

They both burst out laughing.

**

"Shut up, just shut up, Sudha," Sudhir shouted.

"I am fed up of your short temper, Sudhir. I just want to give up now," Sudha hurled back, while sobbing profusely. "If not me, at least think of Shashank, he's just two years old, what impact will such behaviour have on him?"

"It seems my behaviour and I are causing you both a lot of trouble! It is better I leave." Sudhir hastily grabbed the car keys and rushed out of the house, slamming the door behind him. Sudha, broken by the whole episode, did not even attempt to stop him.

In the wee hours of the morning, Sudha got a call on her telephone.

"Do you know Sudhir Awasthi?"

"Yes, he is my husband. What happened?"

"He has met with an accident and we are rushing him to the hospital. Please note down the hospital name and address and come down quickly."

Sudhir did not survive.

Rage and impulsiveness had cost Sudha her happy world. The

biggest culprit, she thought, was the car key.

**

"Rashi, I need to go to the doctor tomorrow for my routine checkup, can you take a day off and come with me?" Sudha said, insistently.

"Ma, I can take you," Shashank intervened.

"Do you have a tight schedule tomorrow, Rashi? We can go the day after."

"No, Ma, that's fine, I can take a day off tomorrow," Rashi affirmed.

**

"I am glad all went well. Your reports look fine, but you need to keep your sugar levels in control, Ma," Rashi said, striking up a conversation on their way back from the hospital.

"Hmm."

Sudha looked at Rashi. She had known the girl for the past 12 years. She has seen her transform into a mature, responsible woman. Rashi had the steadiness that perfectly balanced her son's impulsiveness. She had been an immovable pillar of strength for their family and it was time Sudha gave her another very important responsibility to carry forward, her legacy.

"Rashi, instead of going home, let's go out for lunch. What was that place you and Shashank frequently went to before Shikhar was born?"

"Chillies?"

"Yes, is that restaurant still there?"

"Yes, yes, Ma, it's still very much there. Let's go. I am sure Shashank will be super-jealous when he finds out about this," Rashi grinned.

Sudha smiled back.

**

The duo got into a hearty conversation at Chillies. The old days, fun-filled memories, a few sob stories, all made their way through the warm, rustic décor of the place to their cozy corner table.

"Rashi, sorry, but I overheard your and Shashank's conversation about the key."

Rashi's face turned pale as she recalled what she had said to Shashank.

"Ma, I am sorry, I did not mean that, it was just..."

"Don't be sorry," Sudha interrupted. "By the way, you were right. Shashank should have asked me about the keys, but he never did, and even if he had, he would not have learnt the truth."

Sudha saw a mix of emotions cross Rashi's face, waves of confusion and surprise.

"Let me take you back to when Shashank's father was alive. Sudhir, your father-in-law, was a wonderful man. He loved me and Shashank with all his heart, but his only weakness was his short temper and impulsiveness. Whenever he lost his cool, he would become a different person altogether, unrecognisable. In the early years, I would calm him down, keeping all my emotions aside, but after Shashank was born, I also started having mood swings and my emotions too went for a toss when Sudhir displayed his extreme rage. This does not mean he abused me or tortured me, it was all momentary."

"Just like Shashank?" Rashi remarked.

"Yes, an apple does not fall far from the tree," Sudha said, holding her hand.

"It was that fateful night... Sudhir and I had a tiff over something. We both lost our cool and it turned into an intense quarrel. Sudhir went out in his car and for the first time – or rather the last – I did not stop him. I heard him start the car and drive away in a rush. Shashank was just two years old then and was sleeping inside. I went to him and cried a lot; I didn't know when sleep came over me. Later that night, I got a call telling me that Sudhir had met with an accident. I called my friend to come urgently and look after Shashank while I rushed to the hospital. But before I could reach, all had ended. Sudhir was gone, forever." Sudha's sigh was tinged with pain, as if she had lived the moment all over again.

"Shashank knows his father died in a car accident, but he does not know the reason behind it," Sudha said, taking a sip of water that Rashi had offered her.

Rashi held Sudha's hand tightly.

Sudha continued, "That day and all the following ones would have been so different had Sudhir not found those car keys. He may have gone out for a smoke or slept in a different room or would not have talked to me for days... but he would have been alive. Shashank would not have had this void for his entire life."

"Rashi, after all this, I introspected a lot. When Shashank was 16 or 17, I saw him display the exact same behaviour as Sudhir over a small issue and I had sleepless nights. I had to do something. I spent days seeking a solution, but everyone I consulted thought it was a sign of his youth and said things would change after he grew older. But I could not take a chance. So, I found the way myself. Once Shashank started driving, whenever he was upset or angry over anything, I would just hide the car keys. He would always search for them desperately, in an urge to get out of the situation, but he could not, as there was no escape."

Rashi looked at her mother-in-law in disbelief. "Ma, you were the one who was stealing, I mean, taking the keys?"

"Stealing is the better word, Rashi," Sudha smiled between her tears. "I stole the keys so that the happiness of our family wouldn't get snatched away, again. Here, I want you to take this forward from here and be my co-conspirator," Sudha said, handing over the duplicate keys of their car to Rashi.

Sudha sensed Rashi's bewilderment and remarked cheekily, "You need to be very careful and, as I said, you cannot take a chance."

Rashi gripped the keys and said solemnly, "Count me in as your partner-in-crime, Ma. We are in this together."

**

"Rashi, where are the car keys?" Shashank shouted at the top of his voice after a heated dispute on a phone call with his colleague.

"I don't know, Shashank, they were right here when I last saw them," Rashi replied.

The two partners-in-crime gave each other a small victory smile. Sudha knew her legacy would be taken forward with utmost responsibility.

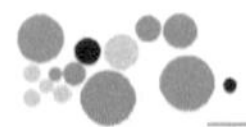

Noopur Joshi Bapat lives in Pune with her husband and five-year-old daughter. A software engineer by profession, Noopur discovered her love for writing early in her school days and runs a blog Kaleidoscope. Besides English classics, she is equally interested in reading Hindi and Marathi literature.

MEMORIES FORGOTTEN

Divya Vartika

I dim the table light so that it doesn't disturb his sleep but the table makes weird noises with every movement of my hands over the cheap notebook I found in the bedside drawer. I am being so careful. Maybe too careful and maybe that's why my hands are shaking so much. Or maybe it is because this is the first time I am sitting with a pen and paper ready to pour my heart out.

How long has it been – four months or five? Maybe it has been longer than that. I don't remember exactly how long we have been on the road. I bet he remembers. I suddenly have a strange urge to wake him up and ask him. I am sure he would not only know how many days but also how many hours it has been since we packed up our basic essentials in our car and drove away. Drove away from our home of the past five years.

We moved into that house right after we got married. And furnishing it turned out to be a nightmare. We had our first fight as a married couple over the colour of the couch. And we had our first make-up sex on the mattress on the bedroom floor. It took us longest to find a bed we both liked. During the initial few months of living together, it seemed we could not agree on anything. I started to imagine that he was deliberately refuting everything I said. But those fights full of passion brought us closer. Maybe we needed some friction to rub off our rough edges and then settle into a more comfortable existence.

He learned to cook. I learned to drive. We both learned not to sleep without resolving a fight. We were happy. We were in love and we were happy. "And they lived happily ever after" – that happens only in fairy tales. We didn't get our ever after. We were happy but it was not for long.

Everything changed in just a couple of hours. Or maybe it wasn't even that long. I don't remember how long they were inside our home. I don't remember a lot about that incident. If I told him that I don't remember, he would say that I am intentionally blocking out the memories. And maybe I am. But what's wrong in that. All I can forget are the details. The pain doesn't go away. I wish I could forget the pain as well. I wish we both could forget what happened to us. It wasn't our fault. We were in our house. We were not walking alone at night in a dangerous neighbourhood. We were inside our home in a safe neighbourhood. The neighbourhood we selected so that we could raise our future kids there. But now, even we were not safe.

After the police went away and the cleaning crew hired by them had cleaned the blood, we both sat in the home all alone. He did not look at me. He didn't look at me for the next three days. I remember that. I also remember when he looked at me next.

We did not speak at that time. Not just to each other but to anyone. Neither of us went to work. We just sat in the apartment not talking to each other. Then on the third night, I found him sitting on the bathroom floor with a blade in his hand. And I didn't feel anything. Nothing at all. It was like my mind did not know the correct response. Maybe there wasn't one. So, I just found another blade and sat down next to him.

That's when he saw me. That's when he actually made eye contact. He kept looking at me for a long time. Or maybe it was just for a few minutes. I don't remember the details. I just remember that his hands felt warm when he took the blade from me. I remember his hands shaking when he threw away the blade in his hand too. And I remember what he said next: "Let's leave. Let's go away from this place."

And so, we did. We resigned from our jobs. Sold our first home along with all the furniture. We just packed our clothes in one bag each and loaded our car. We left my car since it never worked properly anyway. His car was more comfortable. I didn't say anything when he went back and brought our photo album. He didn't say anything when I slipped on his jacket for warmth.

And off we went. We didn't say anything and just kept driving. When he got tired, I would take over. At nights we would find any motel or sometimes sleep in the car itself. Nothing mattered. We just kept driving. I don't remember how much distance we covered from our home. I don't remember if we kept moving in the same direction or if we changed our course. Maybe we crossed the same town more than once. Who cares? I didn't. I know he didn't. All that mattered was just driving.

He loved his music and was proud of the collection he kept in his car. The collection travelled with us. I had heard those songs so many times. Each song was catalogued as a specific emotion for me. Like there was a song that was playing when he kissed me for the first time. Then there was the song that was playing when I saw him crying for the first time two days after our wedding (he didn't want me to see him crying and was hiding in his car). Each song represented something. There were our grocery songs, our going-to-office song, our fighting song. There was a song for every moment we spent together.

But we didn't have any song for this. There was no song for being in pain separately and together. For hurting for ourselves and hurting for the one we loved more than ourselves. No song for the silence between us.

I could feel his pain and he could feel mine. We both were hurt by the same people in the same manner. And we both didn't know what to do next. We didn't know how to handle our own grief or how to help the other.

We did not speak because we didn't know what to say. There no words but we were communicating. Sometimes he would hold my hand while driving. Sometimes he would curl up in his seat and put his head on my lap when I drove. He used to love it when I played with his hair. Now all I could do was wipe his tears while I drove.

But we were healing. It was slow, but we were healing. He would stop the car if he saw beautiful scenery. Then we would sit in one place for long and keep staring at the sky or the river or the forest or whatever had made him stop. Watching sunsets soon became a routine. Wherever we were, whoever was driving, we would stop and enjoy the sunset before moving forward.

Sometimes if the night was clear, he would keep driving through the night. He would never let me drive after dark. I don't know what his logic was but I never objected. We barely talked. I didn't want to waste any words in arguing.

Then one night, he played the song he had played at our wedding. He kept it in a loop and we kept absorbing the music. After the third or fourth time, he stopped the car and got out. I thought maybe he just wanted to stretch his legs. But he came over to my side, opened the door, held my hand and asked me to dance. And there we danced. In the middle of the night. In the middle of nowhere. Under the stars, just two people dancing to a song. We would have made a strange scene had anyone been there to look at us.

It was the first time after the incident that I saw him smile. From now on, this song would be categorised under 'his smile song'.

We slept in the backseat of our car that night. He held me in his arms that night. We started a new journey towards happiness that night.

We started speaking again. At first, we would say which song we wanted to play next. Then what we wanted to eat. Then one day, during our sunset ritual, he spoke about the incident that we never talked about. He told me how he was hurting, what he was feeling. He was patient when I told him what the pain was doing to me. We sat there in the same spot talking from sunset to sunrise. Then we found a room in a motel and made love.

We kept talking over the next several days or maybe even weeks. The details still did not register in my mind. But he was with me now. We were travelling together now.

We found a beautiful bed-and-breakfast in some small town and decided to stay for a few days. It started to feel like our second honeymoon.

The room was nice but some of the furniture was not very stable. The desk in the corner threatened to wake him up. But I wanted to pour out these words before he woke up. I needed to record this day. I had missed my periods for the past two months. When I told him, he held me so gently like I was a china doll that could break from his touch itself.

We went to the town doctor together. We received the news together. We were together when my doubts threatened to rob our happiness. Logically, I knew this would be his child and not a result of that incident. It had been too long and I did get my periods in the months after that. But my mind was too busy being swallowed by fear to process logical arguments. I was glad that he was with me to guide me out of that fog of fear and doubt.

He said that we needed a home now. We couldn't keep on driving with a baby on the way. Neither of us wanted to go back so we decided to go forward.

Tomorrow, we will go on the road again but this time with a purpose. We need to find a town, we need to find a job, and we need to build a home again. And in all of this, we need to stay strong and not let fear control us.

Tonight, I need to write this down to remember. I forgot many things but I don't want to forget this. I don't want to forget any details now. I need to write before he wakes up.

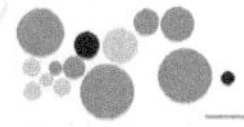

Divya Vartika is an introvert who lives in a small town somewhere in India with her husband. She is an avid reader with a vivid imagination. Her training as an IT engineer along with an MBA degree, and even a decade-long stint working in IT and cybersecurity for companies like Accenture and Deloitte, could not kill the storyteller in her. Currently, she is a full-time writer.

DREAM

Sangeeta Das

The mushroom smiles.

I look at the photo, satisfied. Just the click I need for Instagram. The monsoons bring out the best in all hill-stations. The green cover around me calms my overworked city nerves; the smell of the wet earth feels therapeutic. I can feel the stress of my insane, deadline-driven, corporate, single, 30-something, unhappy life melt away. The chill in the air is warm to my worn-out senses. The birds chirp, the orchids on the trees sway in the gentle wind. I close my eyes as if to hold the moment.

"The leeches must be feasting on you by now," says a voice behind me.

The word leech is enough to bring out the athlete in me. I jump, kick in the air, run a few metres, and almost throw my fancy mobile phone, shouting bitter nothings.

A tiny voice laughs, and I notice my intruder. A small freckled face looks at me, hands inside a huge furry jacket that almost covers the little being who stands with the air of a confident adult but can't have seen more than seven or eight years of existence on this earth.

"Looks like you get scared easily," the lopsided smile betrays his age.

"Anybody would, right, with a stranger creeping up from behind," I say, somehow irritated by the way the kid is trying to make me feel foolish.

I start walking and sense him walking behind me. We walk silently for a while.

"So, what is your name?" I ask without looking back, just to break the silence.

"Rohitesh."

"Seriously? That is a nice name, though it's a very formal one, *Rohitesh*." I stress on the name and laugh, though I regret it immediately – it sounds stupid to laugh at somebody's name.

"Why do you laugh? That is what everybody calls me in school, and you should call me that too, okay?" he says firmly.

It is a command that is also a little pleading; it sounds endearing. I smile, turning back to look at him.

"And what are you doing here alone? It's quite a lonely stretch of road."

"What do you mean alone? I am always on my own. I do all the chores at home when my parents go to work. I know everything,

I am very smart," the kid looks at me with an expression so defiant it almost pierces me. He is not amused at being treated like a kid.

"Ha, ha! Of course you are. So, what do you do, Mr Rohitesh?" This interests him, and he takes a few big steps to walk alongside me.

"We have a huge apple orchard; it has lots and lots of apple trees. They produce bright red apples almost throughout the year. The sweetest apples you will ever taste and the juiciest. My brother and I pluck them and bring them to be packed in the cane baskets. My mummy and aunts make the best apple jam you would have ever tasted in your life. I stick the stickers on the bottles. They are called Rohitesh Jam."

He takes out two apples as he speaks and offers me one. We eat in silence for a while; it is indeed sweet and crunchy. I look at the kid walking with me, his rosy cheeks competing with the apple in his hand.

"You know, we have a few peach trees too. I planted them last year and they will be able to produce fruits by next year. Father got some sheep a few months ago and they poop across the apple farm. I don't like it so I need to shoo them off to the other side of the farm. I like running behind them when they *mehhhh* in unison. I do not like their smell, though, but mummy says they give milk for me to drink in the morning, so I try not to smell them too much now." He pauses as if trying to ward off the smell in his nose.

"So you are a tourist?" He looks at me a little more closely to check if I look like one.

"No, I am from Dehradun, I came to attend a wedding of a relative. Now that the wedding is over, I drove down to Mussoorie to spend a quiet day by myself. They are too noisy, these weddings, you know. And sometimes you are so lost in the crowd; sometimes even known faces are nothing but a crowd and it is claustrophobic. Sometimes you need nothing but peace, away from people, from work, from friends, from the unproductive life you are living."

He nods as if he understands 'the peace' I want. I don't know why I am even telling him all this but it is good to talk to somebody who at least pretends to understand.

"It is very quiet at my apple orchard. I study my books sitting under the big shady trees. Sometimes the bees disturb me with their humming noise, but that's all that you can hear there, the bees and the birds. I like these sounds now, I read about them in my books, so I listen to them." He makes a humming sound and we both laugh.

"My mother made me a swing this summer out of her sari, between two apple trees. It's a beautiful orange swing; all my friends fight to sit and sway on it. But it is my swing and I get it whenever I want." He smiles innocently. I do not interrupt his monologue and we walk along together, sharing the moment. I can see the swing in my mind amidst the apple trees.

"It's been raining a lot these days, so I am unable to go to the orchard. But every morning I look out of my window and see the rain-washed shining red apples. Mummy puts a huge chunk of apple jam on my bread for morning breakfast – it's very funny when I have that jam and look at the apple trees, because the apples look so big and strong but mummy mashes them and makes jam out of them."

I smile, it is funny the way he says it, I can taste the sweetness of the jam as I listen to him. Rohitesh Jam. I should buy one, I think, though I do not really like jam and not apple jam, for sure. Apple has never been to my liking in any way, other than the chunks in my sangria.

The smell of freshly roasted *bhutta* makes me realise we have reached the market at the end of the road. It reminds me I am hungry too.

I look at my little friend, "How about a corn?"

"You get better one on the other side of the market," he tells me with an air of experience, like a father tells his child.

"*Arre*, Chinnu, you are here! Your mother has been looking for you for so long now, go run home!" The tea stall guy shouts at my little companion. "She came here at least thrice."

The boy looks visibly embarrassed at being addressed by his pet name. I chuckle and want to call him "Chinnu," but check myself before being rebuked by Mr Rohitesh.

"*Bhaiya*, give two *bhuttas* and do select the soft ones."

Before I can complete my sentence, my newfound friend leaves me as suddenly as he appeared. I see his figure disappear out of sight as he runs into one of the narrow lanes, probably leading to his home by the beautiful apple orchard.

"*Kya kahe*, madam, his mother always has to run behind him. Growing naughtier by the day, this boy."

I laugh. "He's a nice kid, bhaiya; he kept me company and saved me from the leeches."

Old wrinkled hands roast my golden corn and I settle myself on a small bench beside the tea stall.

"Yes, he's very talkative. Everybody here pampers him. He's a spoilt brat now, but very helpful and an intelligent kid." The old man speaks fondly as he flips the corn.

"He was telling me about his apple orchard and the jams they produce. I was actually thinking I should buy one of his Rohitesh apple jams."

The old man laughs a hearty laugh. "*Arre*, madam, so he told you too about the apple orchard. That is the one he dreams of, day in and day out, since the time he knew to dream. His father is a carpenter and his mother works as a helper at an apple farm. Chinnu loves apples and jam and he dreams of having his own orchard someday. He talks about it so much, it's almost as if he is living his dream."

I am stunned. Not once did I feel it was just a story, I could see the orchard when he described it to me. I could taste the sweetness of the jam that he ate in the mornings. I could hear him running around the apple trees. How could it all be something that he just created in his mind?

I munch on the corn, the apple orchard vivid in my mind.

I pay the old man a fifty-rupee note. "*Bas*, ten rupees, madam," he fiddles to gather the change from a rusted steel box.

I thank him for the delicious corn he chose for me.

As if reading my thoughts that are still on the little kid, he tells me, "Madam, what is life without a happy dream of our own? It is only in those little worlds we weave that we can live how we want and have what we want. Some strive to realise their dreams, and there are some just happy to live in one. Either way, that is the beauty of a dream." He smiles and hands me the change. I bid him goodbye.

His words ring in my ears. "What is life without a happy dream of our own?"

Do I have one? Have I strived to realise one?

I meet my driver at the parking lot on Mall road.

It is past dusk as we drive through meandering hairpin turns. Below, the city lights up like a happy mandala glowing and making its presence felt in the darkness of the night.

A little ahead, we come across a bakery on the side of the road. It has a board with an inviting picture of a hot cup of coffee. I make a pitstop here and get coffee for myself. As I turn to leave, I remember something and walk towards the counter.

"Can I also get a bottle of that apple jam, please?"

*Biochemist, bibliophile and travel enthusiast **Sangeeta Das** was born and raised in the beautiful hills of Shillong, Meghalaya. She is now a learning and development professional based in Bengaluru, and is on a new journey exploring her writing skills.*

AN AUTUMN LEAF

Ruchika Verma

Neglect can be relieving.

I wonder if autumn feels that way. A lot has been written and said about Delhi's ruthless winters and scorching summers. Few people, however, pay attention to Delhi's autumn.

It does not really last that long, but that does not mean it does not exist. It is that one season nobody writes songs or poems about, perhaps a meme here and there – *do we wear the woollen jacket or the cotton T-shirt? Decisions, decisions* – while ignoring the way trees change colour with the relief of neglect.

While most of us pick up a leaf from the ground, click a picture for Instagram and abandon it right there to get stomped on later, seldom do people look up to admire the very tree it has fallen from. While deciding what to wear, seldom do people stop to enjoy the crisp air that they think exists only in foreign countries. Autumn is a season of neglect and that is why I love it.

I long to be neglected, to be ignored, to be left alone to my own devices. I long to be that abandoned autumn leaf that is free to sway whichever way it wants, ready to be stomped yet resilient enough to keep moving in the breeze. I long to be away from my roots, adrift.

Alas, that is not my life.

My feet and the road are together a love story that is always left incomplete. It never finds resolution. They are always star-crossed lovers trying to meet in secret to steal as many embraces as possible whenever they can. It is the final kiss for today, I think warily as the car honks at me. I look up, my father is impatient.

"Get in, quick."

Delhi is one big city that never rests. Even at the most eerie hours, there is someone out there having the time of their lives and I know it because I long for those moments that make living enjoyable, not just bearable.

For someone who has never been allowed to go out on my own, I do have few fancy ideas about how life likely is for those who dare to venture out alone, in the light or the dark.

It must be exhilarating, I think often with a sigh because I am not destined for the adrenaline rush that saves more than half of my generation from the dreaded monotony of life.

College was supposed to be freedom; turned out, it was only a temporary escape. My father drops me off to college and wastes his lunch hour to take me back home. I tried telling him he doesn't have to, but he wanted to be there for his little princess. He could not see her becoming a peasant eating dust, or rather a queen, with a mind of her own.

My family is quite modern, but my parents are protective of me, maybe too much. I used to revel in that, in being the envy of all other children in the school and playground. I was the kid with my mother in tow, not a maid or nanny. I was the kid who talked about sex with her parents and knew already what others learnt much later from porn.

I had the perfect life until one day I stepped out of the bubble and realised I didn't.

It was not a perfect life; it was a sheltered life, bubbled up with nothing but the solid foam of restrictions. In their openness, my parents had made sure to close me up in a castle so high that Rapunzel's hair fell short.

I wish I was a rebel, but I have not a single bone like that in my body. My friends think I do not have a spine altogether. What am I supposed to tell them? I have a spine but it is more rubber than steel?

Maybe I should just bunk college for a day, what would they know? But I never had the guts; it was equivalent to breaking their trust. The close relationship I have with my parents has made me sensitive towards the notion. They bring up the word often, not realising that in their trust of me was hidden a massive distrust – they did not trust me enough to leave me alone.

It is another one of those autumn days I love. I look at the leaves and the way they go from one place to another, anywhere the wind takes them. None of my friends notice it, but I only have eyes for that one leaf. Neglected but free.

I sometimes wonder if I am a thankless brat. A spoiled, pampered mess of a princess. I know I am more. But who is going to tell that to people who think I am simply too entitled and a prude?

The leaf falls near my right foot and I pick it up.

"Hold it still!"

A click, then a second click. At the expense of restraining that leaf, my friend got a picture that would light up his feed.

I let the leaf go; it drifts away, taking a part of me with it.

I have to get that part back, I think determinedly, possessed.

I stand up and start walking away from my friends, following the leaf. I do not hear what my friends are shouting behind me, I do not care when I leave the safe compound of my college, I do not realise how far from it I've come until I stand there, still, looking at the leaf now lying dormant among others.

It is the park where I've been plenty of times, yet this is still my first visit. It is the first time I am alone on my own.

I look around, a scrawny boy whistles at me. I am startled; this has never happened before. He scans me from head to toe, as if undressing me with his eyes; he wolf-whistles again. I feel extreme shame, so much so that I am frozen. I stand there, wide-eyed like a statue ready to be pooped upon by the pigeons.

This is totally different from all the times I've been out with my family. I almost regret it. What have I done? Where am I? Who am I?

That guy is still looking at me. I am clueless. All these years I've been taught so many things, but never, ever, how to deal with a situation like this. I look down unable to bear the sight of his lecherous eyes on me. What if he approaches me? What if he attacks me? What if I become the next headline? The thought makes my knees weak.

As if on cue, something stirs on the ground. The leaves are moving. Then I see my leaf. It is starting to drift again.

I hear a whistle again; a shiver runs down my spine. I look at that despicable boy and decide to ignore him and follow my leaf – my saviour.

I follow my leaf and soon I am out of the park. I look back, afraid. The boy does not follow me. Maybe I am not worth his efforts. Or maybe moving ahead was all I needed to do.

I follow my leaf; slowly but surely, it is moving forward. Then it falls in the middle of the sidewalk, alone and desolate. My exploration comes to a halt too.

Now, what am I supposed to do? I can't stand in the middle of the sidewalk and wait for it to move. It may make sense to me, but people around me will think I am insane or, worse, lost.

I look around, pretending to search for something, but honestly, all I do is pray for the leaf to start moving again. Show me some direction; bestow me with a path to move forward on.

Move, get up, drift away. Do something. Move!

I put all my energy into that leaf, willing – begging – it to start moving so I have a direction. Without it, where am I supposed to go? I have never been out on my own before and without this leaf guiding me, what am I to do?

I wish my parents were here; they were always there to guide me.

Then suddenly, just like the wind that gushes past me, slapping me harshly on my cheek, and still failing to move the leaf, realisation dawns on me.

This leaf is what my parents were supposed to do with me. They were supposed to guide me and then leave me be. They were supposed to let me run to the edge of the cliff, they were supposed to let me decide if I wanted to jump or stick to the ground. Sure, they could hold me back if I decided to jump but they needed to give me a choice first.

A man passes me hurriedly, shoving me on his way, "Get moving, this is not a place to stand."

It is not.

I decide to leap. I enter the first shop on my immediate left.

I glance back at the leaf; it is still not moving but it has moved me.

I have entered an antique store. It is dusty, rusty and ancient. A salesman asks me if I am looking for something, if I like something, want to buy something.

I wonder what money I have, not much. I never needed much. My expenses are limited to canteen food and the occasional stationery. I have some emergency cash, I think. I have never used it without my parent's permission despite it being my own savings from the routine.

I nod awkwardly. I have never done this. I look at a necklace; the locket has a tree with leaves falling engraved on it. As if gauging my interest, the salesman speaks up, "It is just five hundred rupees."

I feel it is too much but what am I supposed to do? My mother always takes the lead in these matters. I have seen her bargaining but I have never done so myself; could I now?

I look nervously at the salesman. And I decide it is time to jump.

Two fifty

Four eighty

Three hundred

Four hundred

Three fifty

Okay, take it.

And I do. I know I bargained the wrong way. But it is the biggest bargain of my life for it is the first. I wear the necklace and get out of the shop. The leaf is no more there.

I look at my phone: eight missed calls from my father. It is an hour past the time he is supposed to pick me up.

I call him back, and I receive the dressing down of my life. I tell him I will find my way home. He demands I tell him where I am. I argue – I have never done that before. This is a day of many firsts. After ten minutes of bickering, I relent, telling him where I am.

I wait twenty minutes out in the cold for him. We drive home in silence. I cannot tell if he has been worried about my absence or angry with my disobedience.

When we reach home, he opens the door and is about to say something when he looks at the necklace on me. Nobody discusses anything that day.

Next day, he drops me to college again. When it is his time to pick me up, he isn't there. Only a text message: *Can't make it, find your way home.*

I smile, clutching the locket. I make my way home; there is lots of pushing, shoving and cursing but I make it home. My parents' faces are pensive but they still smile. That leaf changed everything.

My spine is indeed rubber, bendable but unbreakable.

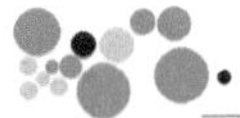

Ruchika Verma is a literature student whose heart lies in the classics. Always seeking fun and ready for philosophical discussions at all times, she wrote her first novel Yes, I Ran Away! *at the age of sixteen, and works part-time as a PR specialist for a technology firm.*

JALEBI

Raina Lopes

Grey clouds filled the sky. The news had forecast a heavy shower. Blue lightning was followed by thunder, but the words still rang loud in Aisha's ears. She was inconsolable and scared of the storm that was about to break in her life. She cried bitterly sitting in a small corner inside her bedroom. Gathering the strength to stand up, she walked towards the window. The clouds could unleash their burden on the earth but, after what had occurred that morning, she had no one left to share her burden with. Everyone in college eyed her with judgement. Even her best friend Riya believed that it was her fault.

It was a regular evening in Chandigarh. She watched people return from their mundane jobs, tired and listless, sometimes stopping to enjoy delightful sips of hot tea at Ramu *chacha's* stall. A new sweet shop had come up across the street in the *mohalla*. A paunchy man with a soup-strainer moustache sat at its entrance roasting bright orange *jalebis* in bubbling hot oil inside a large wok. As soon as they turned crisp, he strained them out and dropped them on a platter. Simultaneously, with a skimmer in the other hand, he dipped the fried *jalebis* in sugar syrup. At that moment, Aisha felt everyone's life was sorted, unlike hers. Melancholy crept inside her heart. Just as she was lost in observing the process, the *jalebi*-maker looked up. Whether he saw her or not, she suddenly felt conscious. She quickly closed the curtains and leaned against the wall beside. What if they spot me? She had nightmares of people peeping at her window and the flooding thoughts maddened her. She grew restless and wished the world would stop. Taking a sharp breath, she opened her closet. The new leather handbag her aunt had got her from London lay intact inside. Rummaging inside the bag, she found the silica gel sachet and held it in her clammy cold palms. It bore instructions in bold printed letters: THROW AWAY, DO NOT EAT. This could help her to escape the horror she had been going through. She decided to mix the white crystals in her glass of water resting on the nightstand. The dirty stares from her classmates and the distraught faces of her widower father and her brother, who were her only family, flashed in her mind continuously.

**

Suraj rushed up the stairs to the terrace. His grey shorts revealed hairy limbs, and his jersey T-shirt was drenched in rain and sweat. He clenched the smartphone tight in his hand, electrified, waiting to open the link that Mudit, his friend from his coaching class, had sent him that evening. His teenage hormones gushed through the blood in his veins. Making his way towards dry space, Suraj leaned against a wrought-iron ladder and unlocked his phone. He quickly clicked on the link. The corrugated tin roof made a thunderous sound as the torrent hit with ferocity. Suraj stayed glued to the screen. At first, the video quality was too pixelated to see clearly, but as soon as the video loaded fully, he could make out the face of the girl who was stripping her clothes one by one until her body was completely bare. He couldn't believe his eyes. Reality hit him, and his face blanched. He closed the tab, tapping the screen fiercely, and went running downstairs to face his sister inside the house.

**

"Come on, Aisha! Be grateful that I am dating you despite your uncountable flaws. Just look at you! You are far from a diva, and without me, you would be facing rejections from suitors just like that fat cousin of yours," Karan said disdainfully over the Skype video call.

Aisha was ashamed of herself. He was not the same boy she had met in the third year of art college. Karan used to be sweet and gentle; he never mentioned her obesity or criticised her for it. But he had completely changed now. She started feeling bad about her body, and began to believe his words. It was true that her cousin Dolly was still unmarried, waiting for her prince charming. Aisha felt perplexed. She surmised that maybe giving in to Karan's demands would bring back the spark in their relationship, but she was wrong. A wild belief and blind faith sucked her into a dreadful furnace of treachery. She could not see through his vicious grin and fake promises.

"Aisha, you start undressing, or I am hanging up the call, and this relationship is over," he snapped at her.

"I will... I will," she stuttered with quivering lips, hands trembling as she unhooked her dress. As every garment slipped down her body, her self-esteem ripped away part by part. Tears trickled down her chubby flustered cheeks, her face was pale, but he grinned ear to ear as he discovered her naked frame on the computer screen. Her bare mounds and flab hung loosely over her stiffened plump form, and her shoulders drooped in defeat as she stood in front of the tiny ball of webcam. The cold tingled her burnished soft and creamy skin, glowing in the white light emitted from the screen. Karan gawked with lust-filled eyes.

**

The flare of her long dress trailed in the breeze. She felt strange stares on her as she passed a group of boys in college. She was taken aback when one of them tried to touch her inappropriately, the rest breaking out into raucous laughter. She felt mortified. From a distance, Aisha spotted Riya and called out to her. Riya glanced at her once and then averted her gaze. Aisha ran towards her and greeted her. But Riya replied, annoyed, "Please stay away, Aisha! I do not want my name to be tainted along with you." Aisha felt stupefied by her remarks and wondered what was wrong. Then she noticed others eyeing her, or glaring at her. She was frightened. Soon enough, she found out that her video call with her boyfriend had been leaked, her shame broadcast on the internet.

She confronted him and was aghast when he ridiculed her publicly, defaming her and defiling her character in front of his buddies. At that moment, she realised that she had made a fool of herself, blindly trusting him while all he did was take advantage of her for his filthy needs. People had always body-shamed her for her weight, and now they had an additional reason to jeer at her.

**

Aisha failed to mix the silica powder in water as she could not gather the courage to snatch her own life. Throwing it in the dustbin, she sat on the edge of her bed, swinging back and forth anxiously. The thunderstorm raged outside, and dusk had settled over the sky. Just then, violent bangs erupted on the wooden door of the bedroom. She was terrified. She slowly opened the door, and it flung open with immense force as her brother stormed inside. His eyes were red with anger, his nose flared as if he was about to kill her.

"What is this, Aisha?" he demanded, holding the phone in front of her. She was sure that he meant her leaked video, but she pretended to know nothing. She hoped that it had not spread across the city like wildfire. She hoped her brother was mad at something else.

"How could you do this, Aisha? You have brought shame to our family. Dad has been sweating day and night for both of us and this is how you repay him? Stripping naked in front of the whole world? Have you lost your mind?" He ruthlessly attacked her with unkind words, neglecting to mention that he too enjoyed watching such videos. But this time, the fact that it was his sister stung him.

"Trust me, *Bhai*. I did not intend to hurt anyone. I never agreed to do such a thing willingly. I am a fool. I am sorry. He betrayed me," she broke down at his feet.

Suraj clasped her arm. Aisha twitched in pain.

"Who betrayed you? Why did you do this?" he demanded an answer.

Aisha narrated the whole situation to him. As the light of truth dawned, Suraj believed his sister and felt sorry for her. Remorse washed over his face; he felt ashamed of watching such clips himself. Boys like him were responsible too, taking advantage of their girlfriends to showcase their exploits to others. Aisha's nails dug into his wrist as she held him tightly. She was scared to face the world.

"You need not fear, my child. Not as far as I am with you!" Her father's heavy voice boomed in the room; he had been standing at the door all the while. He had overheard their conversation as Aisha revealed the truth to her brother. Aisha ran sobbing into his open arms.

**

She slumped against the cushion, stretching her arms up in the air after publishing her new blog post. She had now grown to be a renowned influencer who wrote against body-shaming and promoted self-love. Having won multiple beauty pageants and titles being a plus-size model, she felt confident. She looked at her reflection in the dressing mirror and marvelled at how far she had come in the journey called life. Her reverie broke when the doorbell rang. It was the delivery boy. "Madam, I have your parcel," he said. She frowned as she had not ordered anything. The phone beeped a message. It was her father who texted, "Congratulations, *beta*! You have crossed one million followers on your blog. You'll receive a surprise parcel. It is my treat."

She had overcome her phobia of the internet. What had once

shattered her life into pieces was now her strength. She ruled people's hearts and inspired girls just like herself, who once hated their bodies or those who had been betrayed in love or those who had been denounced by society. She was an independent woman. Opening the packet, she discovered pulpy orange *jalebis* emitting a sweet aroma. She remembered that awful day when she wished for someone to rescue her life from its blazing turmoil. It did happen, as her father saved her, held her hand, and helped her back on her feet. Her family didn't give up on her. They put up a strong front and battled society. Karan was put behind bars after she gathered the courage to lodge a police complaint. The decision to move to Mumbai helped her restart life away from toxic neighbours and gossipers. She learnt how to strengthen and protect herself – emotionally, physically, financially, digitally. Her perspective towards her body also took a different turn. No girl deserved to be violated and humiliated for trusting the wrong boy, just as no girl deserved to be shamed for looking different. She inspired women to love their imperfect bodies and lives, just like the crooked yet sweet *jalebi*.

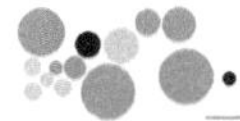

Raina Lopes works as a software engineer at a renowned multinational company and is a writer at heart. She loves spending time observing the serenity of nature and finds solace in reading.

THE NIGHT OUT

Sapna D Singh

It was well past midnight and she was dog-tired, but sleep eluded Ela. After tossing and turning for a couple of hours, she pulled aside the duvet and went to the adjoining bathroom. She splashed cold water on her face and looked into the mirror. "Oh dear, is this me?" She stared at the haggard face with sunken eyes and grey hair over the forehead and temples. She wanted to cry aloud, but she bit her lip as she did not wish to wake Anand up. He needed to have a good night's sleep otherwise he would have a migraine in the morning and of course he had his office to attend to the following day. "Ela!" She was startled and rushed back to the bedroom. "What on earth are you doing with the light on at this hour?" Anand asked her.

Ela saw a shaft of light coming in from the bathroom door, so she quickly went inside the washroom and switched off the lights. "Now that you are up, go and check on Ma," he told her brusquely and went back to sleep.

Ela nodded and trudged towards the hall. Once outside the bedroom, she counted till ten and took long breaths to prepare herself for what she would encounter tonight. Across the hallway was an extra room that had been converted into a bedroom for Anand's mother. The other bedroom was occupied by their daughter Nyasa who was studying in class ten. Ela quietly opened Nyasa's door and saw that she was fast asleep.

She tiptoed towards Ma's room with trepidation. Bracing herself as she gently pushed open the door, she felt nauseated by the strong stench emanating from the room. Ma had again soiled the bed and Ela would have to spend the night cleaning up the mess. Exasperated and frustrated, she stepped closer to the bed but Ma was not there. Her heart missed a beat and she almost fainted. "Oh, now what," she said to herself.

For the past two years since Ma had been diagnosed with dementia, life had changed for the family. Not that it was a bed of roses earlier, what with daily reprimands from her then healthy mother-in-law and an indifferent husband. But now, she was tired mentally, physically and emotionally.

Shaking her head to remove all those thoughts from her mind, Ela checked Ma's bathroom but it was vacant. Then she remembered the last time this had happened. Ma had opened the main door and stepped outside at midnight; they were lucky that the society guard had seen her and brought her home.

Ela shuddered as she recalled how Anand shouted at her and complained that she was not taking good care of his mother. Ela wanted to tell him that her life had been devoted to the family, which was why she had left her promising career at an airline to be a homemaker. But Anand was no longer the man she had married. He had turned into a stranger and she was staying in his house because she had nowhere to go. Moreover, there was Nyasa to think about.

"Should I wake Anand," Ela pondered, then discarded the idea. As expected, the main door was ajar. She went out and luckily found Ma standing indecisively in the corridor. Ela heaved a sigh of relief and caught hold of Ma's hand. "Who are you? I want to go home," cried her mother-in-law.

Ela gently took her by her elbows and nudged her towards their apartment. Once inside, she saw Ma's sari was all wet with urine. Ela took her to the bathroom, bathed her and draped her in a fresh sari. Then she cleaned up the bed and put Ma to sleep after giving her a sleeping pill.

She took all the sheets and clothes to the washing machine. She could hear the call to prayer from a distant mosque and gathered that it must be four in the morning. Today was the fourth day in a row that she hadn't slept a wink. She remembered her friend Neeta telling her to hire a nurse to look after Ma because she needed professional care. But that would require money and Anand was not in favour of keeping a nurse. "What are you here for," he said. "It is your duty to look after her," he told her.

Life had become drab and mechanical these days – just cooking, cleaning and nursing her mother-in-law. "God, when will it end?" she wondered. She was not cold and unkind but she was exhausted physically and mentally. She thought she had become spiritually depleted too because sometimes she wished for her mother-in-law's death to free herself from the daily ordeal.

Then came Covid-19, and Ela's life became even more difficult. She didn't have many friends and her social life was non-existent in any case, but she missed her morning walks that had stopped due to the pandemic and Ma's deteriorating condition.

As the drum of the washing machine started to swirl, Ela's mind went over yesterday's incident when Ma did not recognise Shobha, her sister-in-law. Shobha was upset and shocked to see her mother like this and Ela was also heartbroken.

After a few minutes, Ela went once again to check on Ma who was fast asleep. She took a fluffy white pillow from the bed and as she was trying to put it under Ma's head, it slipped from her hands and fell on Ma's face. It happened so suddenly that Ela didn't know how her hand started to press the pillow on Ma's face as she lay motionless due to the effects of the sleeping pill.

The washing machine beeped outside just then and Ela jumped back. She threw the pillow away, her body shaking and her face pale. She felt so weak and unstable that she collapsed on the floor.

"Ela! Where is my breakfast?" Her husband's voice woke her up. She glanced at her mother-in-law and felt terrible, berating herself for what she had almost done. Ma was still sleeping. Ela put her hand out to check Ma's breathing and felt elated when she found her alright. After adjusting the bed sheet and duvet, Ela went straight to the kitchen. It was already seven a.m. and Anand was getting ready for work.

Ela quickly took out two eggs from the refrigerator and started making an omelette. While her hands were busy, her mind replayed her horrendous act. She never thought of herself as Mother Teresa but she could not think of hurting anyone either. However, what she had done to her helpless mother-in-law proved that she had a violent streak. "Am I such a bad person? A criminal?" she wondered.

After giving breakfast to Anand, Ela warmed milk for Nyasa who was also sitting at the dining table discussing some school project with him. Ela could not look them in the eye even though they had no clue of what had transpired in the other room. A guilty conscience pricks the mind, Ela thought.

"Come mamma, sit here," Nyasa said lovingly, but Ela gave her a weak smile. Anand, as usual, did not even bother to look at her. "If he knew that I almost killed his mother, he would become a mad man," Ela thought to herself and shuddered involuntarily.

"Give Ma's medicine and food on time," Anand said to her and put on his face mask as got up to leave for office. When he was out of the main door, Ela heaved a sigh of relief, letting go of the sense of suffocation his presence inflicted on her.

Nyasa was back in her room talking on her phone. Ela went back to her own bedroom; she wanted to lie down and sleep but she had loads of pending household chores that needed her attention. While fixing the bed sheet, the incident with her mother-in-law started to replay in her mind. She started shaking. "I am not evil. I am not evil," she repeated. So engrossed was she in her thoughts that she didn't notice her daughter standing in the doorway. "Mamma!" Nyasa yelled. Ela jumped like a startled rabbit and turned around to face her daughter.

"What is wrong? You are not your usual self today. Has papa fought with you again?" Nyasa asked all her questions in one breath. Ela was touched by her daughter's concern and for a moment she decided to confide in her. But then she stopped herself. "Nyasa is a kid. She cannot be burdened with these things and, moreover, she might start hating me for being so callous," Ela thought.

She hugged her daughter and said she was fine. "I am simply tired. I am going to sleep now. You please go and study," Ela said, gently pushing her daughter towards the door. Nyasa was reluctant to leave but she knew her mother too well. She was a private person who did not share her secrets with anyone.

After Nyasa left the room, Ela quietly went to her mother-in-law's room. Ma was still asleep, possibly due to the impact of the sleeping pill, Ela thought. Ma's face looked serene and still. For a seventy-four-year-old, she looked young despite the illness she had been living with for the past two years. She was a proud woman in her heyday as Mrs Meeta Singh, a teacher in a government school. Ela sometimes felt that even after retiring from her job, the teacher still resided inside her. Ela remembered the long agonising lectures her mother-in-law used to give her, which included the duties of a wife and daughter-in-law.

Looking at the hapless woman lying in front of her now, Ela felt only pity for her. For the past two years, Ma had become a shadow of her younger days. Nowadays, she was dependent on Ela for the smallest of things. Ela had to be alert all the time to keep an eye on her. Ma had not just forgotten people but she was losing the sense of who she was. She could not identify herself and had started to forget basic things like turning the tap on and off. The other day she urinated in the balcony. Initially, Ela was sympathetic and patient but gradually she had become tired and overwhelmed as she had to manage everything singlehandedly without any break.

Suddenly, Ela sensed something was amiss. It was Ma's face. Ela had never seen it so calm. As she bent forward, closer to the face, she was astounded. Ma was not breathing. A panicky Ela checked her wrist but there was no pulse.

She embraced the body of her mother-in-law crying with grief, fear, guilt and relief.

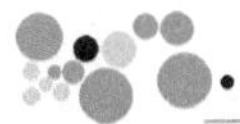

Sapna D Singh is a journalist with two decades of experience in both Indian and international publications, including some of the biggest media companies like The Times of India Group, Indian Express Group, Business Standard and S&P Global Platts. She has covered myriad sectors ranging from healthcare to energy and from corporate affairs to textiles.

THE RESURRECTION

Urvashi Tandon

Sudha absentmindedly caressed the leaves of a palm placed next to the sofa in the room of the company guesthouse as she reflected on her visit to the office earlier today. A copy of *Garden Spaces* magazine lay on the centre table with her image smiling for the camera against the backdrop of a lush, landscaped garden on the cover.

She had headed straight to the head office in Versova upon reaching the city from Pune. Her cheerful disposition added as much a bright spark to the office as her yellow sari that looked remarkably crease-free despite the long drive. They wanted her to handle the landscape design for their planned township and new office in Panvel. She felt very proud of the fact that she had been chosen over the local professionals in Mumbai and was aware that the landscaping she had done at holiday homes in Lonavala and Karjat must have been noticed as there had been rave reviews. Of course, being featured on the cover of a highly acclaimed magazine was another feather in her cap.

The meeting with the CEO was very pleasant up until the moment that the Assistant Director Finance was called in to discuss funding of the project. Suresh had walked in very briskly but had stopped in his tracks when he saw Sudha. She was caught unawares too! A floodgate of memories swamped her, and she was nonplussed for a moment, but quickly regained her composure.

She was all of 25 years of age, a devoted housewife and the mother of two girls age three and six when Suresh had come home one day and announced that he was tired of her and the responsibilities that he was burdened with. He demanded a divorce out of the blue and she was devastated. They had a love marriage with the love having disappeared within the first five years. She learnt later that he was having an affair with a colleague at work. Sudha was an immensely proud woman and did not ask him for financial help. All that she got from the marriage was their house in Pune and a financial lumpsum amounting to three lakh rupees.

She was in her first year of college when she met Suresh and eloped with him and so there was neither degree nor work experience to talk about. Her family had disowned her and now she had two little girls to look after and no means of an income. She was completely broken and could not figure out how she would come out of this mess. What she lacked in education, though, she more than made up for in grit and determination.

The girls kept her going and she derived solace from her hobby of gardening. The plants in her little garden were her sounding boards. They heard her troubles and sorrows while comforting her as she spent several hours amidst them. Her world having crumbled around her, she could not trust anyone anymore. These plants were non-judgemental, and she was blessed with green fingers. Soon, there were little saplings and seeds that she had collected and dried. She experimented with herbs and even they thrived under her care. Her friend Shivani came up with a brilliant suggestion one day as she collected a few saplings from Sudha: why not enrol for a garden competition in the neighbourhood? The activity brought some excitement into Sudha's life. Shopping for garden artefacts brought her tremendous joy and the garden was shown off with great pride when the judges came visiting. She won the competition and the meagre cash prize of five thousand rupees was a boost to her morale. She went on to win several more such competitions, which gradually progressed to contests at larger scales as her skills improved.

She was approached to conduct workshops and soon her saplings and seeds were put on sale at a nearby nursery as well. She was hired as an adviser at a local gardening centre and her clientele began to grow. Soon her field of work expanded from little gardens to doing landscapes for private properties and then larger commercial establishments. Interviews and accolades became her steppingstones and her fame and fortune grew over thirty years. And here she was at this juncture, reflecting on her tough but satisfying journey.

There was a knock at the door as a steward brought her a much-needed cup of tea and some cookies. She was asked whether she would be staying for dinner or would be meeting friends in the city. That made her smile. Yes, she knew someone in the city who had once been very close, but she would not categorise him as a friend. She said she would dine in and asked for some soup and salad at eight o'clock. Once the steward left, she reflected on her feelings for Suresh. What did she really feel when she saw him today? She was a little surprised when she realised that he did not mean a thing to her anymore. She thought all that pain and anguish she had gone through would have left a feeling of resentment, anger or even hatred, but there was no trace of any of these emotions. She was grateful that he had walked out on her. She would never have realised her full potential and would have lived a very ordinary life of a traditional, devoted housewife. It was good that he had not once tried to contact her or find out about the girls. She may have just wallowed in self-pity and grief had that happened. She loved and valued the freedom she had. She also basked in the knowledge and confidence that comes with being a self-made successful entrepreneur. She was grateful to the Almighty for having allowed her to expand her roots. Had she been confined in a stifling marriage, she would have grown like a stunted plant akin to a Bonsai. Allowed to spread her roots in loose soil, she had grown into this large tree that people looked up to and some even revered. Friends and well-wishers like Shivani and a few others had provided the right nourishment and environment for her to blossom. She smiled contentedly, secure in her sense of self-worth. She put down her empty cup of tea and decided to step out for a stroll before it got dark.

After a change into comfortable track pants and a T-shirt, she put on her walking shoes and headed out. At fifty-five, she was still attractive and made heads turn as she walked past the reception area. It was a well-kept guesthouse with a little lawn outside, which was unusual in the city of Mumbai. Outside the gate was the usual hustle and bustle of a busy street in the city. She decided to explore the area and turned left. The guesthouse was in a residential area but there was a busy market with colourful, well-lit shops and crowds of shoppers at the corner of the street. She walked on for some time, but the traffic and the noisy crowds soon made her uncomfortable. A car whizzed past blaring its horn and startled her, so she decided to turn around and retraced her steps. As she walked the quieter length of her street, she reflected again on her current situation. Tomorrow was a scheduled onsite meeting with the architect who was planning the township and later in the day, a meeting with the finance department. Would she encounter Suresh again? She shrugged indifferently. They were just working on a project and beyond that there was nothing to talk about.

She entered the gate and noticed a little red Santro parked to the side. It hadn't been there earlier. As she approached the reception desk, she was greeted by the receptionist with a message that there was someone here to see her. Surprised, she turned around. Suresh was seated in the lobby area waiting for her. She could tell he was awkward meeting her like this. She apologised for her attire and asked if he would care for something to drink. As they waited for the order of coffee to materialise, Suresh asked her about how she and the girls were doing. She could not help but wonder if he even remembered their names. She replied that they were all very well, and deliberately did not divulge any more information voluntarily. "Fancy meeting you like this," he said. "Yeah, life does spring surprises," she replied. He went on to tell her that he had married the girl he was involved with and they had two children, a boy and a girl. She smiled politely. The coffee arrived and a heavy silence followed. They really had nothing to say to each other. "What made you drop by?" There, she had finally said it!

He fidgeted with the handle of his cup as he looked askance and said, "I was surprised to see you and thought I should congratulate you on your achievements." She looked at him shrewdly before countering his words. "Oh, come on! It certainly cannot be that or you would not have remained silent for thirty years. You didn't look back or check on us even once in all these years so you might as well tell me the real reason you are here." Suresh was taken aback. This sharp retort would not have come from the Sudha he knew. Here was a strong woman who was sure of herself. "No one knows at work that I was married before," he blurted.

She looked at him pitifully and wondered what she had seen in him to have run away from home with him. "Don't worry. They won't know from me and, by the way, there's a lot I need to thank you for." He looked perplexed as she smiled and said, "It was because of you that I took my first independent major decision when I eloped. It was again thanks to you that I was forced to step out into a very competitive world where I floundered and fell but rose again and achieved all that I have today as a completely self-made woman."

Coffee done, she excused herself, "I have an early start the next morning and it was a tiring long journey today, so I would like to turn in early for the night." Suresh stood up and she extended her hand and shook his, saying it was nice to meet him, and she wished him good night before walking out of the lobby.

Dr Urvashi Tandon *is a professor of anaesthesiology. She served in the Indian Navy for 29 years before seeking premature retirement. She has written articles for various magazines and has authored a collection of short stories for children titled* Potpourri – Stories for Children, *which aims at creating environmental awareness in the younger age group.*

MOONDUST

Anushree Bose

Gauri Didi loves the colour blue in a way most girls love a bar of Cadbury. She painted her bedroom walls cyan. She is always wearing her Prussian blue jeans dungaree with edges beginning to fray. Her passport panel is Oxford blue and the paled pages within bear stamps in inky blue. She keeps a navy blue faux leather wallet, which is fat with green American dollar bills. Whenever Gauri Didi is visiting, Maa takes her to Nattu kaka's convenience store instead of me to carry home bags of lentils, rice and spice sachets. While middle-aged, ill-humoured and balding Nattu kaka weighs cooking oil or salt, his unblinking beady eyes super-glued to the balance scale, Maa casually interjects that Gauri Didi is visiting from the *America*. Then, she elbows Gauri Didi, a cue to dazzle an unsuspecting audience. But nobody is ever impressed by Gauri Didi's English because she doesn't *sound* American. Maa thinks it is embarrassing to live in America for three whole years and not pick up the accent. Baba thinks Gauri Didi's unchanged vocal inflexions reflect her patriotism, her true-blue Indian spirit. I have no interest in Gauri Didi's accent but I do feel bothered by other things, like how she has cropped her hair like a boy's, how her nails are cut too short and seldom painted, how she refuses to wear a sari and doesn't wear makeup, how sometimes she sneaks in a whole crate of cheap beer and takes noiseless sips at night over Baba's unbroken snore wafting from the living room, mere inches away from her!

Gauri Didi is nice to me but sometimes I wish she goes back to America and stays there for good. I had fervently wished her disappearance just two days ago on my birthday. Maa had cooked Indian food – a boring curry and meat pilaf – that Gauri Didi likes to eat; no pizza, no cola and no deep-fried savouries. Baba bought the weird and salty cheesecake from the Paradise Confectionery at the wastefully expensive Mall; it had tasted like hardened custard. Baba forgot I had wanted the same chocolate cake from the nearby Amma's Bakery that all of my friends had had for their birthdays. Everybody was weird. My friends didn't want to play games or dance to DJ mixtapes; they wanted to talk to Guari Didi instead, like adults gossip at get-togethers. The stereo was turned off and tube lights were flicked on. My friends gathered around Gauri Didi and they touched her in the way people touch pretty precious things at the museum's exhibit when no one's looking. They wanted to know about her American friends and the American way of life. What do Americans eat? Do they always have pizza, pasta and burger? How lucky! What do Americans do when there's load-shedding? Do they dance in the rain and float paper boats in potholes? Are there potholes in America? How come Americans have such fair skin and flawless English? Gauri Didi had cackled with amusement and called them all 'sillies'. Her face shone with a subdued pride as if American lifestyle is in some way her labour of love. She said most Americans are white but dark-skinned people like her are American citizens too. This raised eyebrows. Potholes are rare, she continued, and there is no load shedding as there is enough electricity for everyone, but during maintenance work, there are scheduled power cuts which are duly informed to the residents in advance. In between her little speech, she carefully sipped water as if it were steaming tea. How weird! She reasoned Americans speak flawless English because it is their mother tongue just as Hindi is ours. She informed us Americans are street-smart, even confident but not necessarily intelligent; many have drug problems or do petty crimes to get by. Many Americans do not finish school and they do not 'have to' go to college. In America, farmers, plumbers, electricians, florists, carpenters, chefs and seamstress make enough money to live well; they do not have to be a doctor, engineer, civil servant or lawyer to afford nice things.

After her lecture punctured a hole through my friends' enthusiasm for the American life, Gauri Didi took many selfies with me and my friends on her humungous mobile phone named after a dumb fruit. She complained I look dull. She needs smiling pictures to email to her vibrant American friends. "They must not think India is a sad little country!" she had insisted emphatically. My friends thought her oversized mobile phone was very cool though its screen had a big ugly scratch. They didn't know it had been purchased from a hair braiding salon in America that was also an illegal thrift shop dealing in stolen electronics, quite conveniently only three blocks from the Indian restaurant where Gauri Didi works. In America, Gauri Didi attends an art school by the day and every night she works for a Bangladeshi man – Mr Salim Siddique from Sylhet, who runs The Mustard Mahal restaurant. Instead of taking orders from customers and pushing the fish about to go bad, unlike the other girls her age waiting tables at the restaurant, Gauri Didi assists Mrs Siddique and two of her helpers in the dingy kitchen. She deftly guts the fish, deveins the prawns, marinates the tender mutton cubes and fat chicken thighs with spice mix, chops several kilos of onion and grates at least three coconuts every evening in preparation for the dinner menu for the night. By the time the restaurant is teeming with local patrons whom Mr Siddique often regales with fabricated stories of wars, malaria and Hindustani music on request, Gauri Didi is out of the backdoor with her share of the restaurant's rejects like fish's head, tail and eggs. Using these and some frozen or canned vegetables, she fixes herself a stew to be had with boiled Rosematta rice. In America, she is barely noticeable but over here she is a demi-goddess who hands out cheap Statue of Liberty key rings and *I heart NYC* fridge magnets to our relatives and neighbours, subtly rubbing into their weathered faces an out-of-reach lifestyle.

Gauri Didi claims that talking to people gives her the migraine, then why was she such a chatty-Cathy at my birthday party? Everything around her had glowed as if she were the pale orb of Moon scattering softened light into our bleak existence. I had taken comfort in knowing she will be leaving for America the next weekend, this is why I was shocked when I returned from school to find Gauri Didi indubitably gone and my parents distressed over her abrupt disappearance. Maa kept looking under the bed, inside the almirah and cabinets every few minutes, as if Gauri Didi is a misplaced saucer or shawl that is still very much in its intended place but Maa has somehow overlooked it. Baba has been making phone calls since morning, Maa told me as she sauntered around the room, attentive like a wild cat, ready to pin down Gauri Didi the moment she decides to emerge from hiding. Maa didn't have to tell me Baba has been smoking too since morning, and if there is no news of Gauri Didi he may drink illegally brewed country liquor at night. Only months ago people died from drinking bootleg alcohol from those backstreet distilleries in our district. I tried to feel worried for Gauri Didi, but I couldn't; I instead felt my tongue sour with bile and rage. After practising all day for the upcoming inter-school sports tournament, I was just too exhausted to care. My growling stomach took me to the kitchen where I foraged for food that wasn't there. But I stumbled upon something even more precious. Gauri Didi had left sticky notes on the left side of the rusting refrigerator that barely cooled anything these days. If one didn't look around, the notes were easy to miss. She is leaving for America early, one of the sticky notes informed, she will explain later why and she is truly sorry. I didn't buy this. She could be anywhere really, shacking by the sea or hitchhiking to the mountains, seeking her fill before she resumes her menial life overseas. But my parents will believe her because right next to her shoddy apology, another sticky note read, "Get a new fridge." She had stuck several thousand rupees bills to the fridge with a garish souvenir magnet that was also a bottle opener. What a sassy exit, how American!

I took the sticky notes and the money to my beleaguered parents. They were relieved, of course! In their eyes, Gauri Didi hadn't run away tossing the family name into irretrievable shame, she hadn't been kidnapped against her will, she hadn't walked out on them yet and she still seemed willing to keep this sad little house afloat. I was relieved too. I finally had Gauri Didi's absence to keep me company. I made myself a bowl of Maggi masala noodles and went to my room; it is mine again, now that Gauri Didi is not around. The room is too small, the size of a decent six-seater dining table and it has a small window high up the wall which doesn't open but lets in ample sunlight through the frosted glass panes. I plopped down on the musty bedding on the iron cot that groaned ominously under my weight and gave in to glorious sulking. In between mouthfuls of piping hot Maggi, I finally undid the cellophane-wrapped box, strapped with curly ribbons – the birthday gift from Gauri Didi. It held a secondhand smartphone, black and boring, just like hers but without the ugly scratch. I hate this but I will use it anyway, at least until I buy myself a firsthand phone. I will probably gift Gauri Didi something good that isn't refurbished. In the golden light spilling into the room, my skin glowed like a sequinned fabric. I could picture myself soaring high! I am fast on the tracks; I could secure a sports scholarship. Sports academies have better turnout than art schools anyway! I will train hard with the best coaches from the country in the swanky stadiums of Delhi. I will have the sculpted thighs of star athletes and wear white shorts that flaunt my becoming calves. My speech will be accented, like a native English speaker. I will settle in the suburban wilderness of Australia and have kangaroos roam about my backyard. I will be special and important: adored, admired and envied! I will throw money at my parents who will approve of me in ingratiating silence. I will gift useless gadgets to my neighbours whose eyes will pop out like buttons. I will have exotic stories to tell ignorant little children used to the filth of slums. Nobody will remember or believe that I used to be one of them...

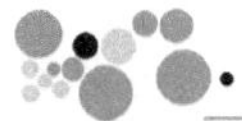

Anushree Bose *is a clinical researcher and a DBT-Wellcome Trust India Alliance fellow. She has a PhD in psychiatry, a Master's degree in psychology, and specialises in the scientific study of mental disorders like schizophrenia. Beyond academics, she likes to read, write and wonder about human nature, something she explores through poetry and fiction.*

AT HOME, FINALLY

Arva Bhavnagarwala

Bombay, India, 1990

Stepping out of the railway station, eighteen-year-old Rehana gawped at the sight before her. "This is Bambai?" she asked her husband, Aslam, while clutching his hands for dear life as he attempted to navigate their way across the busy road. He grunted in response.

They boarded a bus; Rehana squealed in excitement as the giant red box moved towards her. Sitting down, she voiced her thoughts aloud, "Where are we going? Where is our house? How big is it?"

Aslam looked at her scowling, "Be quiet. You'll see everything."

His scowling face didn't dampen Rehana's mood. "Look at that," she said, pointing to a tall building, "Do people live there?"

Aslam chose to ignore his new bride. After a while, he motioned for her to stand up. Grabbing their luggage, he walked towards the exit, Rehana following him like a puppy.

She stepped down from the bus and her eyes widened like saucers. Stammering, she managed to say, "Wh...what is this place?" She couldn't take her eyes off the pure white structure in the middle of the sea. She had heard about the Gateway of India and the boat rides of Bombay, but no one had told her about this. For a moment she thought Aslam was taking her to the place in front of her. But instead, he crossed the road and began walking in the opposite direction. "Listen Asla..." she began, then remembering her aunt's advice of never calling her husband by his name, she cleared her throat, "*ji*... You didn't tell me what that place was."

Aslam grunted again. "I'll take you there later." He was a man of few words, Rehana realised.

Running to keep pace with her husband, she couldn't stop thinking about her new house. Would it be huge like the one in the village? Would there be a verandah? But before she could imagine any further, they came to an abrupt halt. She didn't realise they had turned in a narrow lane; there were rows of huts on either side, leaving only a small space to walk. After a few steps, Aslam opened a lock to one of the huts.

"Are we going to rest here? Then you'll take me to our new house?" she asked.

He looked at her with his eyebrows raised. "*This is your new house.*" He laughed at her dumbfound expression. "What did you expect? You will live in a palace like a queen? This is *Bambai*, a city in which we have to struggle for a place." He dumped the luggage and stormed out.

Looking around the hut, she wondered how two adults could even sleep together. And where would she cook? Where would she wash herself? She felt drops of water falling on her hands and realised she was crying. Her tears came like a waterfall and her body shook with sobs.

Hearing her, a woman walked in. Hugging Rehana, she murmured soothing words, "It's alright. Ssshh… stop crying, dear."

Rehana gazed at her through her tear-stricken face and whispered, "Thank you."

"My name is Farida, I live next door." The woman patted Rehana's head and left.

As exhaustion kicked in, she curled herself on the floor. A fitful nap later, Rehana woke up, thinking she must be dreaming about her horrid surroundings. But she was in the same place Aslam had left her. The tears started again as she remembered her village. Her parents had passed away when she was young, and her uncle's family had raised her, given her a primary education, promised to marry her in a good family. Her aunt and uncle had painted rosy pictures about this city. How excited she was to come here! Rehana hadn't expected this. Their betrayal stung. But now, she didn't have a choice.

She arranged her belongings in one corner. The shanty had no ventilation, only one door. She kept the stove outside and planned to cook there. Her village seemed like a distant dream.

***

Time passed. She never had the chance to visit the monument that she had seen on her first day. She later learnt it was the Haji Ali Dargah. Her trips were limited to the end of the lane for filling water and using the common bathroom.

A year later, she gave birth to her first child. She named her Reshma. Her husband didn't look happy. He had changed jobs, first as a butcher's assistant and now selling clothes on the footpath. He often came late in the nights, with his gait unsteady, speech slurred and a weird smell wafting around him. It was not until Farida told her that she understood her husband drank too much alcohol.

"Do you have money?" He garbled to her one night.

"No, Reshma *ke abba* (Reshma's father), from where will I get money?" she answered.

He slapped her and snarled, "Do you talk to your husband like that? No manners. Bow your head and talk to me." He dragged her out of the house. The slum dwellers had gathered to watch, but no one interfered. This was a daily occurrence; someone or the other was always fighting. Only she didn't imagine it would be her turn one day. "I want you to start earning," He started yelling again. "Beg on the streets if you want to, but I want money. Am I clear?"

Rehana hiccupped with tears and said the first thing that came to her. "But, Reshma *ke abba,* what about our daughter?" Another slap hit her face.

"Reshma *ke abba,*" he imitated her. "Kill her if you can't take care of her. I don't want her. Or better yet, take her with you to beg. The rich will show some pity and throw a few rupees."

Rehana tried to reason, "You are angry now, let us talk in the morning. Please."

"How dare you disobey me? You don't want to beg, get out of my house."

"But... you don't know what you are saying, *ji...*"

"You ungrateful woman! You don't want to leave the house? I'll leave it then... *Talaq talaq talaq!*" He stormed out of the lane. The onlookers gaped at his retreating form, while Rehana felt her world spinning around her before she fell onto her knees.

***

"What should I do?" Rehana asked Farida, two days after that dramatic night. She had managed to call her aunt in the village and told her what happened. Her aunt consoled her but also subtly made it clear she was not welcome back.

She stared at the empty containers of rice and flour, and looked at the little hut that gave a roof over her head. She couldn't bring herself to call it home yet. Her tears had dried and she knew that crying wasn't going to help solve her problems.

She looked at Farida, who was now her best friend and confidante. "There is work at the place where I go. They need a maid for scrubbing floors and bathrooms." Farida was in her thirties, a widow and had managed to survive this city. Rehana knew she could survive as well.

"Yes... yes, I'll do it." Rehana held Farida's hands in gratitude.

A new chapter started in her life. Every morning, she took her daughter with her and diligently fulfilled her job duties. It wasn't enough, though. She couldn't take up more work because other employers didn't like a baby wailing in their homes. Her employers gave her clothes. But she had to feed two mouths.

She visited the Haji Ali Dargah often; it gave her strength to carry on living the way she did. She longed to take the famous boat ride. "We will, one day," she looked at her daughter and promised.

***

December 1992

One morning, a few men gathered. Rehana pulled open the door a little to hear what they were talking about.

"The Hindus have destroyed our Babri Masjid. We will not stay quiet. Our brothers from Dongri are planning something. Let's go and help them."

Although Rehana did not understand much of what they were talking, she didn't like it one bit. She felt her heart beating fast and her palms turned clammy. She hugged Reshma, who was trying to stand using the water drum as support.

News of riots breaking out in the city spread like wildfire. People were scared. Farida reassured her, "Don't worry, there's a curfew outside. When they release it, we will buy milk and food." Rehana nodded. A sense of foreboding engulfed her. The days passed but the riots continued.

One night, there was a frantic knock on the door. "It's me, Farida. Open, quick."

Rehana gaped at Farida's dishevelled state. "Hurry, we need to leave." Rehana grabbed Reshma as she heard screams coming from the end of the lane. "They are here, they will burn us. Run…"

They pushed their way along with the crowd. Men, women and kids were screaming. She clutched her daughter close and ran with the others. She didn't know how long they were running when they reached a railway line. "Let's get to the other side. It's an entirely Muslim area, we will be safe there," Farida came up to her, panting.

When they reached the other side, they saw a huge fire rising from the area they had left moments ago. A few women screamed. Rehana found herself unable to move, but the others pushed her forward. She couldn't get it out of her mind. "It's alright. As long as we are alive, we can rebuild everything," Farida managed to say in a steady voice.

But Rehana knew and so did the others, their life wouldn't be the same when they returned. If they returned. She wondered about her little house, whether it still stood.

They stayed on the footpath on the other side with their Muslim brethren. Rehana often sat with a distant look in her eyes. "What is it?" Farida asked her one day.

"I was thinking about Reshma *ke abba*."

"Leave it, don't think about that coward. He must be married to someone else or lying in a gutter. Who cares?" Farida said.

Rehana looked at her and shrugged. "Maybe. I never really knew him. We only had a physical relationship." Scoffing, she continued, "This marriage and this city have changed my life..."

"Mine too," Farida concurred.

***

As news spread that the riots were in control and curfew was being lifted, Rehana hoped she could go back. She voiced her thoughts to Farida. "Are you mad? That is the only Muslim lane in a predominantly Hindu area. We can never go back. Because if it happens again, they won't spare us."

"But I want to go there. It is the only home I have." She had tears in her eyes, but she was smiling. She had acknowledged the hundred square-foot hut as her home after two years.

They agreed to return and maybe retrieve their belongings, if they remained. With trepidation, they retraced their steps back to the slum.

Some huts were burnt, some crushed but a few others remained untouched. Rehana ran with Reshma and Farida. They stopped in front of their doors. The huts remained intact, to their immense relief.

Rehana pushed open the door and looked around her little house as if she was seeing it for the first time. She touched its rough, unpainted walls and wept. Turning towards the west, she paid her obeisance to Allah, thanking Him for showing mercy on her.

A few women came, telling her to go back.

"I'm not going anywhere. This is my home," she told them with a flinty stare.

Rehana knew she would have to endure many things in this cruel world, but she also knew one other thing. This place would remain special to her as long as she lived. Hugging her daughter, she smiled and wiped her tears.

She was at home, finally.

*Based in Mumbai, **Arva Bhavnagarwala** is a paediatrician by day, writer by night and a struggling mother to two boys. Her writing journey began in 2016 and since then her stories have been published on various platforms and in anthologies. Besides writing, parenting and her work as a doctor, she loves to read, travel and exercise.*

YOU ARE ALL MENIALS!

Priyamvada Singh

"What do you mean he's missing? How can a thirty-year-old man just walk out of his house barefoot?"

I was discussing fabric procurement with the team when my cook Chanda called to share the disturbing news. Dashing out of the meeting to avoid them overhearing, I accidentally dropped a few textile samples. I am usually not so clumsy – but nothing in my life seems 'usual' anymore.

Picking up the scattered fabrics, my colleague Geetu offered to book me a cab. I responded with a forced smile, dangling my car keys at her. I was trying hard to retain a composed exterior. After all, no one likes people who carry family problems to work.

But then, pushing my hair away from my face, I felt beads of sweat trickling down my forehead. Heavy perspiration in a centrally air-conditioned office had exposed my anxiety. Slipping the car keys back into my desk, I nodded a weak yes to Geetu.

It was a long drive home from the suburban district where my workplace was located. I sat in the cab, flipping callously through a catalogue. Procurement was the last thing on my mind, but digging my face into a work-file was the only way to avoid the cab driver's snooping eyes judging my teary-eyed face through the rear-view mirror.

Staring at the upbeat mood-board of our new garment collection, I felt even more downcast realising that there was no one I could reach out to at this point. My parents and Jayant's mother lived in their respective hometowns, and there was no point getting them worried till I had something substantial to say.

Scrolling through my phone, I realised that even though we had been married for almost a year, I still didn't have any of Jayant's friends' or colleagues' contacts in my phonebook.

The two of us were introduced through family about eighteen months ago, and agreed to get married after a few meetings. Jayant is a graphic designer based in Delhi just like me, and both our families live in Rajasthan.

He had chosen an elegant café for our first meeting. He was polite and well-mannered even though a little reserved. He frowned upon the idea of sharing one's life on social media – something I agreed with him to an extent. Being a creative professional himself, he understood the requisites of my job as a senior merchandiser in an export house. The unconventional work dynamics were not an issue with him.

When I wrote the pros and cons of this relationship (yes, I did that), I felt that his introvert nature could possibly act as an obstacle between us, especially because I was no social diva myself! Had I been a little more outgoing, three years of independently living in the national capital would have definitely resulted in more than just a few awkward dates – the failure of which eventually led me to allow my parents to seek a match for me.

Since the ticks on my checklist for Jayant surpassed the crosses, I decided to take the plunge. Our initial months together were not rosy like the quintessential honeymoon period, but they were pleasant. Jayant often carried his work home, and I had my hands full working on a new consignment for Europe. Our lack of zsa-zsa-zsu concerned me occasionally, but it was an arranged marriage between two shy people – it probably needed more time to blossom.

One evening, Jayant announced that he had taken a few days off from work. Days turned to weeks, and Jayant turned into a sloth who never left home. He refused to talk even after a lot of persuasion, so I decided not to be a nag and wait till he was ready to open up himself.

A few days later, I chanced upon a hiring alert by Jayant's company for his profile. A call to his office corroborated my doubts. My parents were of the opinion that it was Jayant's male ego that prevented him from telling me about losing his job. They convinced me that things would get better once he got a new job, and urged me to manage the house quietly without putting any pressure on him. I followed this advice for two months, but matters only got worse.

I was eight minutes away from my destination according to the GPS tracker in the cab when my thoughts were disrupted by a bang on the window. There was no way to explain to the insistent teenage boy at the traffic signal that I was not interested in buying his heart-shaped balloons – not today.

Reaching home, I found Chanda only too eager to vomit out the incident and get the burden off her back. "He was staring at the TV for an hour and nodding in agreement – but the TV was off, Saavi Didi! The way he stormed out barefoot, it seemed as though someone had summoned him."

Chanda had been cooking for me way before I married Jayant, and she was never one to mince words. Where could he have possibly gone?

Chanda made several cups of tea after I reached home, but took away each cup untouched. When she arrived with the next cup and turned on the lights, I realised that dusk had fallen and there was still no news of Jayant. I was clueless about whom to contact from his social circle. There was still a lot of time before I could file a missing person's report.

What if he had met with an accident? He had no identification on him. His wallet had remained untouched for days... just like his stack of neatly ironed office-wear.

Suddenly, I heard Jayant's phone ringing. Truecaller revealed that the call was from a multispecialty hospital located ten kilometres away. Jayant had been admitted in their emergency ward, and since he did not have any identification or mobile on him, they were calling the number he had verbally passed on to them – his own mobile number. They confirmed my relationship with him and asked me to come.

As I approached Dr Sen's chambers at the hospital, I was a little stumped. Why did the receptionist send me to a psychiatrist?

Chanda watched me talk to the psychiatrist through a glass pane. The door was soundproof, but a peek at my face was enough for her to comprehend the gravity of the situation. She held my hand as we walked towards Jayant's ward.

I could hear Jayant muttering something repeatedly. He was commanding the two nurses there to get out of his sight. He was foul-mouthed and rude – a tone he had never used with anyone before – at least not to my knowledge.

I finally reached face-to-face with the man I thought I knew. As I called out his name, his uncompromising eyes turned towards my direction, reflecting a reality I had vehemently denied while dragging myself to this ward.

"You are a menial. Do you hear me? You are a menial." This was clearly meant for me. "You are all menials." He included the nurses and Chanda in this classification.

Dr Sen signalled the nurses to step back and waved the ward boy to step in. Jayant observed and seemed to approve. "I consent to your rule here. That's the order from the supreme." Jayant was clearly exhibiting delusions of grandeur. They were making him believe that he was someone special and that he possessed some superpowers.

Shrouding my fragile emotions under the cloak of composure, I pulled out a few questions for the doctor. If Jayant believed himself to be superior, why was he accepting the doctor's orders or being comfortable with the ward boy? Why was he facing issues only with women? How did he walk ten kilometres from the house barefoot in the scorching heat without hurting himself?

"The human mind works in mysterious ways," the middle-aged doctor began on a philosophical note. "Jayant's feet had developed severe blisters and he had fainted on the road due to dehydration when a Good Samaritan called our helpline. Since his mind was overpowered by the false belief of supremacy, it shut itself to the physical pain."

The gender-aversion, according to Dr Sen, was a strong lead to probe further into his condition. Over the next few days, Jayant remained at the hospital, and I was joined by my parents and Jayant's mother.

Jayant had been hearing voices in his head for the past few days. These were auditory hallucinations that were sometimes derived from external objects as witnessed by Chanda when she saw him interacting with a switched-off television.

Dr Sen's team conducted separate interview sessions with me, Chanda and Jayant's mother for added perspective. I was also asked to gather specific information from a few of Jayant's work associates.

As the pages of Jayant's past were dusted, the picture became clearer. He had grown up in a family where gender stereotypes were ground into his psyche as intensely as the spices that his mother painstakingly hand-ground each morning because his father did not like the taste of the mixer-ground chutney!

His mother's sessions revealed how her late husband and the men of the house were so privileged as to sleep in the only room with a cooler during summer; how it was an unsaid rule that women would always eat their meals after the men were done, even if it meant that the main dish would be regularly polished off by the men alone!

Incidents like these are common across many households in India. How was it that it affected the psyche of some more than others? "The human mind works in mysterious ways," the doctor was philosophical again.

Jayant's subconscious had always positioned him on a higher pedestal because of the gender power-play he witnessed in his growing years. When we got married, my independence gradually began to challenge his masculinity. However, seeing me as the caregiver who heated his dinners on nights when he worked late, always ordered his favourite dessert over mine at restaurants, and insisted that he drive the car whenever we went out together made him secure of his machismo.

His colleagues spilled the beans about a demanding female client who constantly turned down his designs. Her overriding demeanour irked him to such an extent that he quit a job he genuinely loved. The reason he could not confide in me was because he saw me in the 'opposite' camp. His severely reclusive nature had not won him many friends, and he could not even post his rants on social-media handles because he did not have any.

His sense of defeat against a woman became the triggering point for his condition, and brought him to a point of extremity where the voices in his head started telling him that "all women are menials". That became his comforting truth.

Dr Sen's treatment made Jayant feel better over time. The doctor also pressed upon the need to induce gradual transformation at home to gently evolve his outlook. "Change begins at home," he said.

This was certainly a life-changing experience, but it brought us closer. Jayant's case was of residual schizophrenia, which meant that he had a past history of one episode but did not reflect any symptoms like delusions or disorganised behaviour later.

Today, we completed twelve years of marriage. There are no major celebrations this year due to the ongoing pandemic. It's just us – celebrating each other.

Watching our daughter Mira climb a chair to hang balloons and son Uday slice the *paneer* into perfectly-sized cubes for the grill, I remember the wise words of Dr Sen, "Change begins at home."

As I smile watching my children break gender stereotypes, I suddenly hear Jayant laughing in the other room – and I do not hear the television.

Priyamvada Singh worked in television across Mumbai and Delhi for over a decade before pursuing her vision of restoring her 150-year old ancestral fort in Rajasthan through her 'Meja Project', which has given the village of Meja a new look, and the rural community a new outlook. She has won various awards including the Nari Shakti Puruskar in 2019 for this endeavour that blends heritage restoration and socio-cultural resurrection.

A FATHER'S DAUGHTER

Bhargavi Chatterjea Bhattacharyya

It is ten minutes past midnight. I am smoking cigarettes alone in my room. My father used to smoke cigarettes and I got this habit from him. My brother does not smoke, but he chews betel leaves. My mother used to chew betel leaves as well. I have lost both my parents to cancer. My mother died two years ago. My father died just seven days back.

We were a small and happy family. My parents, me and my younger brother. How I wish those happy days would last forever! My mother was the best cook in the world and my father was a role model I could look up to. Now I feel my life is a total mess. It started when my brother married against the wishes of our family. Just after his wedding, he left our family home with his wife. They shifted to Bangalore. My mother was worried whether his wife would be able to cook for him. My sister-in-law is a good cook, but it was pointless trying to explain that to my mother. She always felt that her 'young boy' was missing his mother's cooking. I was okay with him moving out of the house, but what I found hard to digest was that he was becoming emotionally distant. Maybe that happens naturally when you get married. Maybe that happens to men. I don't know.

I did not marry. Or maybe, I did not get married. I think men do not marry, women do not get married. I had always been a very independent woman. I worked, I smoked, I drank alcohol at parties. Nobody would like to have a *bahu* like that. Besides, I felt that as my brother lives so far away, I should look after my parents. I owe my life and education to them. They have brought me up like this and I am a capable and confident woman. My parents are proud of me. They depend on me. I think deep down they are sad that their son does not look after them. It does not matter, I am here to shoulder all the responsibilities.

In fact, my decision not to get married came as a surprise to many. My parents found it very hard to accept. They were torn between worry about what society would say and the desire to respect my wishes. The values they handed down to me include strength, independence, freedom of thought. In the end, they decided to let me do as I please. I was extremely attractive when I was young – slim and tall with sharp features. I had big expressive eyes. No doubt, I had quite a few suitors. All of them were heartbroken. Now I am fat and have freckles on my cheeks. I have bags under my eyes and wrinkles on my face. But even then, I hear snide comments at work. They say, "Look at her – the fat beauty." "Even at this age, look at how she dresses up." "She is so proud." Actually, I enjoy hearing these comments. Jealousy is definitely a form of flattery.

But once my brother left home, my mother did not live very long. She had cancer in her mouth. Initially, she had a sore in her mouth. The doctors felt it was caused by vitamin deficiency or some such thing. But the problem persisted. Finally, they did a biopsy and diagnosed it to be cancerous. My father and I decided that we would not tell mother that she had cancer. She would die of fear. But I think my mother guessed something. Whenever she tried to bring it up, we would laugh it away. I used to say, "Mum, you are obsessed with cancer." My father said, "You know the biopsy result was negative. Why do you still think that you have cancer?" But it was difficult to put her off the scent. One day, when we were not at home, she went through all the medical reports and found out that she had cancer.

I remember that day clearly. I came back home from work. My mother hadn't turned on the light; she was sitting alone in the darkness. My sixth sense told me something was wrong. My mother said slowly and deliberately, "Why didn't you tell me that I have cancer? If I had known this even a few months ago, I would have made a trip to Rajasthan. I really wanted to see the golden fort of Jaisalmer. Now my cancer is advanced and it is summer. I will not be able to make the trip."

I have thought about it again and again. Did my mother really want to go to Rajasthan? Is it possible that she felt so strongly about it and neither my father nor I knew? I think she was really angry and just wanted us to feel bad because we hid the truth from her.

Next, it was my father's turn. He had lung cancer. Initially he just had a cough. He himself dismissed it as smoker's cough. But, one day, he coughed up blood. We went to the doctor, who diagnosed it as tuberculosis. So he took medicine for it. But his symptoms did not get better. Then, the doctor asked for a biopsy. My father felt very shaky when the doctor asked for a biopsy. I reassured him that it was just to rule out the diagnosis of cancer. Maybe he just had tuberculosis that was playing up.

But the biopsy confirmed that he had cancer. I was very upset after seeing the biopsy report. "Why me?" I had already lost my mother and now here I was with my father suffering from cancer too. Suddenly, I felt very alone. I cried and cried. Then I gathered courage. I have to give it my best shot. "He is my father. I will do my best so that he lives."

It did not even cross my mind to hide the diagnosis from him. I told my father straight away that he had cancer. This time I had learnt my lesson. I did not want a repetition of what happened when my mother had cancer. But I was surprised to see my father's reaction. He had been the head of the family and I had always known my father as a strong man who could handle anything. But I was mistaken. Now, he looked so vulnerable. I had never seen my father so terrified in my entire life. I saw him cry alone sitting in his bedroom. He thought about death all the time. He stopped eating. He would lie in bed all day and mope about it. The worst part was that he did not talk to me. He became remote. I had always looked up to my father for guidance. Now, I didn't want guidance, but it would have been nice if I could talk things over with him at least.

I told my father not to worry. I would seek the guidance of the best doctor in town. I did thorough research and asked around. Finally,

I decided to consult Dr Ghosh. He is a very renowned oncologist. After a long waiting period, I got an appointment with him.

Dr Ghosh examined my father and went through the reports in detail. My father's face was as white as a sheet of paper. He was trembling. He was waiting for the doctor to pronounce his "death sentence." Dr Ghosh looked up. He said, "Who told you that you have cancer?" In bold letters he wrote on the prescription, "No cancer." Later, he had a quick word with me in private. He gave me a different prescription and said all the medicines for cancer should continue.

My father came out of the chamber a different man. He was smiling. I hadn't seen him smile for ages. He regarded the prescription as a trophy. "I don't have a cancer," he said, beaming. He started eating, he gained weight and he got out of bed. He started to walk. In fact, he even went to the market. He got a new lease of life.

My father lived for six more months. He lived life king-size. This was how I had always seen my father. Cancer could not crush his spirits.

My brother came after my father's death last week. He performed the last rites at the burning *ghat* and the *sradh*. I am a woman, I don't have any rights. I felt hurt. I looked after my father, I made arrangements for his treatment and now that he is dead I don't have the right to pay him my last respects. If that is what the society feels, so be it.

My brother went through my father's papers, his fixed deposits, his shares, his will, and also his medical papers. Then he got hold of the prescription. He was delighted. He said, "This is great. I'll use this for filing a case."

I was surprised. I asked, "What for?"

My brother said, "It is a case of medical negligence. The diagnosis was wrong."

I insisted, "But he had been treated for cancer. Dr Ghosh wrote this just to boost his spirits."

I was in two minds. I said, "Let me ask the legal department at work tomorrow." Tarun, who worked in my company's legal department, told me, "Ma'am, what are you saying? You will just be wasting your time. You have to prove that the patient has suffered because of this wrong diagnosis. But he had been treated as per protocol. There is no case of negligence."

I came back and told my brother what Tarun has said. He laughed again and said, "You and your legal department! Dr Ghosh is a very renowned doctor. Do you think he will waste his time going to the court? He might be able to prove his point, but at what cost? Instead of practising and earning money, he will have to go to the court for several days for the hearing. He will lose money and if this gets publicity, it will damage his reputation. Besides, he has a lot of money. He will pay us cash and sort the matter out. Done."

I have been smoking because I can't sleep. Just two small words, "No cancer." He wrote them deliberately. But those two letters transformed my father's life. He became his old self. His smile came back, his self-confidence came back. I keep thinking and thinking about it. And I go on smoking one cigarette and then another and then another.

Finally I decide that enough is enough. I take out the prescription and tear it into a thousand pieces. I was using my father's lighter for smoking. I now use the same lighter to burn the prescription. Then I go to the bathroom and sprinkle water on my head. Now I am at peace with myself. I have performed the last rites, burning the prescription, and paying him my last respects. I will sleep peacefully tonight. *Om shanti.*

Dr Bhargavi Chatterjea Bhattacharyya is a practising psychiatrist in Kolkata. She was awarded the Morris Markowe Public Education Prize by The Royal College of Psychiatrists, England. After journal and newspaper publications, she recently started experimenting with fiction. Her diverse experiences as a doctor in England and India provide the rich tapestry for her stories.

THE ALLURE OF POWER

Chandrika R Krishnan

I remember the first time you made me go down on you. It was on the eve of Diwali and I was just thirteen.

I was busy gawking at the room – which was big enough to fit my entire home in – and felt you move as fast as the mice do in our house when we unroll the bed and spread it out every night. You held me down as I squirmed, struggled and gagged until you shuddered and went limp like the leftover carrots we get for free from the vegetable vendor who takes his cart around the area. I remember opening a couple of doors till I came to the one that was the washroom and I kept puking till I had nothing more to bring out of my stomach and yet I wanted to heave more. I wanted to pee but I was unsure how to use the throne-like seat, which was like nothing I had ever seen before. I pressed my fingers to my eyes, sobbing all the while, and I tried to wash my mouth to get the taste of you out as much as I could... but each time I only felt like gagging more. I was brought here by my Amma... but where was she? I knew I had to reach her, tell her... We had entered together but I had not seen her leave. Did she call out to me? Why didn't she come back looking for me?

When I finally managed to gather enough courage to come out, I saw you sitting on the bed and the look in your eyes and the way you smiled made me throw up again. I watched horrified as my vomit trickled through my fingers and out onto my dress and onto your multicoloured carpet. I did not know then that it was worth several thousand rupees but it was thick enough to absorb my puke. It was an ugly room with multiple mirrors and heavy curtains and my teacher's quote came into my mind: "There is no need for a real scholar to shout out his knowledge." I couldn't think of any reason why I felt it related to you.

A born orator and a leading debater in my school, words rarely eluded me. Crying, I remember shouting at you and using all those words I never even thought I knew. I let out a stream of expletives that I had gathered from the books that I had read over the years which made their way from the subconscious to the conscious. Spent, the thirteen-year-old me quavered, "I will tell my Amma!" I can still remember your laugh when you said I would be back and turned away as if to dismiss me. Little did I understand the underlying threat, until I was on my way home with my mother in her new car. I also did not know that the trunk of the car was filled with new clothes, sweet packets and firecrackers.

I tried to speak to my mother but she shut me up as always with that 'look' and a warning glance at the driver of the car. My mother was the kind who believed in doing the 'right' thing. Hence, it was sacrilegious for an 'outsider' to be privy to family matters. I slunk further into my seat choking back my sobs, waiting to reach home. Once home, I was desperate to share the experience with her, but before I could speak, she said, "Listen, Kanna, look around you, just see the state of our home, think of your siblings and me. This could be our gateway to affluence. Your father cannot provide enough and with six mouths to feed, clothe and educate, the paltry amount he earns will never take us far."

Stupefied, I had looked at her maniacally blazing eyes and realised that she knew what had occurred and had given her tacit support by willfully leading me to you. In her younger days, she had struggled to make it big in cinema hoping for a break when she fell in love with one of the crew members on the sets. My father had thought the world of her and had actually fought with his own family in his efforts to please her. After giving birth to four children in quick succession, the romance died and along with that her hope – till she saw me as her passport to dream once again, though vicariously. Each time I opened my mouth to resist, she rolled her eyes meaningfully. It was her way of letting me know that my younger siblings were 'too young to know' and I should wait for an appropriate time to speak my mind. I knew that she was buying herself time. She had prepared my favourite pumpkin *halwa* as one would do to appease a sulking child and I gagged. For a second, there was hesitation in her eyes but then she was made of sterner stuff.

My brother and sisters were young enough to enthusiastically celebrate the festival of lights without much thought about the crackers that had miraculously appeared this year. They were also too thrilled to wear new clothes to nay spare a glance at their older sister's pale self and her refusal to come along with them. I looked at my father beseechingly and heard his thunderous words, "I would rather have us beg on the streets than sell my princess!" But the words I heard were merely in my head… and there he sat licking his lips nervously, a man whose ambition could never match the woman he so desperately loved.

My heart broke as I realised that it was the beginning of my end. Surprisingly, I hated him more than my mother. She was truer to herself unlike the man who fathered me.

I caught the ends of my mother's sari, "Amma, you don't know what he did…" Tears streaming down my face, I tried again, "Amma, he… he…"

"You will get used to this. I gave myself to this man," throwing a furious glance at my father, she continued, "for nothing except a lifetime of pain and the four of you at regular intervals. At least you will want for nothing!"

"Amma, how could you?" I tried my hand at shaming her. "How could you call yourself a mother?"

A hard slap was all the answer that I received.

My whimper, "I want to study, be a doctor," went unheard. From her sudden busyness, it was clear that she was in no state of mind to look at other tough options when my beauty and lissomness provided an easier, quicker one. My mother always abhorred being average.

Later in the evening, every house was lit with little lamps to shun the darkness, but for me the vision of the bejewelled you in your gaudy dressing gown dimmed all my lights ever since. It was a week later that you sent for me and my mother accompanied me. If she had any remorse, she did not show it. She felt that, like most mothers, she was doing what was best for me. Years later, I realised that she wanted to climb the social ladder whatever be the means.

As my mother promised, you cherished me and it was because of your patronage that I shone in the world of cinema. True, I was beautiful and I had an innate ambition to perform my best, but the fact remained that the producers didn't want to rub you the wrong way. You loved playing God to all those who treated you as one but I have also witnessed your vindictive side. I was your protégée and you ensured that I knew it. You took care of me so long as I knew my place.

Initially, I was taken aback by the number of people who used to genuflect in your presence, adulate and adore you. You played the role of the charismatic messiah to perfection and it was lapped up by moviegoers who wanted to escape the harsh realities of life. You were a star and never attempted to be an actor. Producers were happy to cast you for they could laugh all the way to the bank and beyond as you set the box-office tingling away merrily.

True to my mother's wishes, my acting career peaked. Major stars vied to be paired up with me, yet I knew you vetted the ones who did and they knew the ground rules. I was rich yet you were the one in control. I grew powerful and you let me grow. I was a queen and could make the moves across the chessboard of life but if it wasn't for you, I had no power. In fact, many hated me for having it all too easy because of you. Isn't life funny? They knew that it was you who called the shots but they hated me because they saw in me their contender instead of a victim. I was questioned about my attitude, my closeness to you... but despite our age difference and the young age I made my debut, nobody believed that the choice wasn't strictly mine. Nobody accused you; rather they resorted to victim-shaming. I wasn't the only nubile girl that you had your way with... though, for some reason, I remained constant, besides your 'long-suffering wife'.

For a brief moment, I tried to break away. I did fall in love with another star and you found out. You ensured that all his films were shelved and he had to retreat. I hated you then but I also knew that I had no way out. The world of movies was like your fiefdom. I had no education, no other means. My siblings had a good life thanks to me. My mother was also happy. My father walked out one day, never to be heard of thereafter. I tried to retain my original self but slowly this new life took root. I never got any true affection and that made me a hard woman.

I grew to like you... maybe, it was the famed Stockholm syndrome. The older you became, my power over you grew and I started using my clout to my advantage. Power-play was quite heady. Slowly, I distanced myself from my siblings. They tried to be close to me not because they loved me but because of my immense wealth. When my mother died, I didn't cry.

**

2018

I browse the net in my tastefully decorated home caught up in the

\#metoo moment. My fingers tap on the key board....

@Thegreatestofthegreat, the GOD of superstars has feet of clay. He molested me @ 13. If not for his 'stroke' would he have stopped his shenanigans?

I ruminate. Doubtless, it will become viral but I wonder if it would impact you now that you are bound to bed. Have I not chosen comfort, convenience and connection over taking a stance? I now have the ability to finance a dozen films and nip a dozen more ideas in the bud if I choose.

The heady flavour of men and women genuflecting in my presence and having producers lining outside my house is addictive. I decide to sleep over it. I stretch looking at my young assistant. Well-trained, he walks towards the bed with resignation and fear in his eyes.

Power is indeed a major turn-on. I have you to thank for that, I couldn't let anyone grow close enough to me.

Chandrika R Krishnan is a Bengaluru-based writer and educationist with 200-odd published articles and stories that are eclectic and mostly experiential. Of late, since the 2020 lockdown, she has taken to learning Sanskrit, gardening, hosting WhatsApp quizzes, storytelling, collecting jokes, and volunteering at a local hospital and Seva centre that feeds the poor.

THE DANCE

Kala Priyadarshini

Even while she was dressing, she had a feeling that the evening ahead would be wonderful; a sense of non-conformity filled the air. She felt she would walk among the clouds once again.

Years of a routine life, home-office-home, of raising a family, of answering questions and ignoring questioning looks, of building up defences... she had done it all. At this age she could, for all she cared, let her defences down and live. For once, for herself.

Ira pulled out the buttercup yellow dress from the cupboard and placed it against herself. Was it too bright? Could she carry it off? She cast aside all doubts and decided to wear it. The yellow stilettos would be too much, so she settled for the more classy black patent leather ones. A matching clutch. She opened the jewellery drawer and stood poring over it. White pearls or dark maroon garnets? She settled on the garnet earrings and necklace and placed her ensemble for the evening on the bed. Satisfied, she looked into the long mirror, which threw back her image: some weight around the middle, some flab on her upper arms, lines on her long neck, deepening laugh and frown furrows, age spots and uneven skin on her face.

She opened the vanity box and reached for the concealer. "The best invention," she thought with a smile and thanked God for creating those who made blemish concealers and skin-tightening creams. She chose a smoky grey eyeliner. Pink or blue eye shadow, she wondered. "I feel pink," she said aloud and began thinking about the pinkness of her thought. Pink was feminine and felt like a woman who had come of age.

She was complete, despite the many half-filled spaces in her life. It was many years ago that she had found herself standing quite alone at the crossroads of life. Sudden singlehood had unsettled her but she had picked herself up and moved on, finding a job, raising the children, and settling them. She was fairly successful and had earned some fame and name. Now she thought she could celebrate. She could wear the deep yellow dress with a low neckline and, without a second thought, wear a sensual scent. She could. Yes, she could live her life.

The ring of the phone jolted her to the present.

"Do you want us to fetch you?" said an excited voice.

"Not really, I will find my way. What time and where?" asked Ira.

"Come early. We are meeting at this charming place called Upstairs on Peter Celli Street, opposite the Santa Cruz Basilica. It serves the most delectable seafood – oyster, crab, squid, mussels, clam... you name it. You will love it. Be on time. Nandu is coming too."

"Oh, is he in town?"

"He was passing by and had called. I asked him to join us. He would love to meet you after all these years. Dress well and wear flowers."

"Flowers? But I am not wearing a sari. I am wearing a dress."

"Wow, that sounds perfect," whistled Rita. "Then I will wear my LBD. See you, dear."

Ira hung up, irritated by Rita's intrusive ways and her constant efforts to pair singles. Rita had this irrational and annoying belief that everyone needed a partner. "Nobody should go to bed hungry or alone," was her standing joke; a bit crass, thought Ira.

That's why she had invited Nandu. Of course, he was part of the group and the school alumni and his place at the reunion dinner was legitimate. But had he not been her junior in school?

Upstairs was indeed charming. A flight of wooden stairs led to a crowded first floor, filled with people from across the world. Rita had chosen a long table by the window. Strings of dolly bulbs hung across the ornate grilles and light bounced off roadside sign posts on to the foliage in flower boxes. Ira walked confidently towards the table and felt a deep blush warm her face as the group welcomed her with a slow clap. Heads turned to look at her and Rita gathered her in a bear hug.

"Oh, my gawd, you look gorgeous. Why don't you always dress like this? So chic, so devastating! Forever hiding behind those drab cotton saris."

"Hush, Rita. Let me meet everybody," said Ira, settling herself between Ramesh and Tara. Ramesh had just retired from a globetrotting corporate job. Tara, Sunil's wife, headed the overseas project of a big hotel group. Ira looked at her classmates and felt proud that each one was a success story. They had had good jobs, settled children, grandchildren, and peaceful retirement homes. They took holidays twice a year… if such things were a measure of success and happiness. Her life had been different, though.

"I have ordered shrimp cocktails for starters," Rita's voice rose over the din. "There's wine going around. Let's raise a toast to Ira. To the return of the native!" Everyone burst into guffaws.

"What do you mean?" asked Ira.

"Rita and her inexplicable ways. She is incorrigible," said Ramesh. "Remember, her essays were never understood by anybody and, of course, Raman sir would be flummoxed by her casual use of expletives." Ira laughed and suddenly wondered if the lipstick she had worn was too dark.

The food and drinks had a relaxing effect. The music stirred people up. "Good feelings are coming," said Tara, taking a big swig of wine. Ira found she was tapping her foot. She was beginning to loosen up when Nandu walked in.

"Here comes the sun…" sang out Rita, "we are all waiting for you. You look swell," she said, rushing forward to welcome him. The years had not cost him anything; in fact, the telltale sign of the passage of time, his salt-and-pepper hair, only added to his suave looks.

Nandu looked straight at Ira. "How can you, looking so beautiful, just sit and listen to the music? It's sinful. Come on and dance."

A Spanish song was playing, pulsating with life. Many didn't understand the lyrics, but it managed to stir everyone. Nandu pulled Ira out of her chair. There was no dance floor as such but he began leading her into a quick square dance.

Ira was dancing after years. In her younger days, she had loved to dance and had learnt all the moves. The music, the wine, the food, the company... it was all too much. She surrendered to the present and began dancing with joy. She moved gracefully keeping pace with Nandu's light steps, following the pressure of his fingers on her waist. As the two danced – sideways, turn around, roundabout, close and near, far and away, forward, backward, pirouetting, cavorting – the years in between dissolved into the surcharged air.

Soon they were jiving vigorously doing the rock 'n' roll. When he led her to do the twist, she found herself managing well on her stilettos, moving her pointed shoes from side to side, even lifting a foot off the floor sideways, in style, and swaying her hips in tandem with the music. Nandu was not faring badly, either, she noticed. The two could barely keep themselves from laughing while they danced.

"Let's do the cha-cha-cha?" said Nandu and began guiding her. "One, two, cha-cha-cha," he said and she responded, "Three, four, cha-cha-cha," carried away on the wave of the beat. A moment from the past struck her and she whispered, "Zorba, you Zorba." "Sirtaki, you mean," he said, and spread his arms horizontally, one across her shoulder and she spread hers, one over his shoulder. The two moved a step to the left and then to the right, crossing their feet. Nandu in a quick hop went down on bent knees, balancing on his toes to rise up with poise. She laughed with gay abandon clapping at the slick performance, feeling a warm flush suffuse her.

The music changed to a slow number and Nandu looked at her as if seeking permission. She allowed herself to be drawn into the circle of his arms, sensing the subtlety of his touch. Diffidently, she put her arms around his neck and their now minimal footwork synchronised like notes in a symphony. A sense of *deja vu* filled her but she forcibly blocked the past. The foxtrot afforded proximity to talk and though Nandu was saying something, she could only smile, overcome by this magical moment.

Little did she realise that they had become the cynosure of all eyes. Each table fell silent looking at the lady in the yellow dress and her partner. Many cleared to make space for their handsome dance.

When the music finally stopped, a thunderous applause rose. Many came up, kissed Ira and congratulated the pair. Ira could not believe what she had done. She involuntarily held her dress up at her neckline and, with the other hand, pulled the hemline down as if she had exposed herself. Nandu grasped her hand and looked into her unsure eyes.

"That was fantastic, Ira. You were wonderful. The years have not taken away anything from you. On the contrary, you have become better like vintage wine," he exclaimed.

"Oh please," said Ira. "Don't say any more." She caught the

excitement on Rita's face who winked at her. Ira cringed and Nandu laughed loudly still holding her hand.

"Come on, folks, that was super," their group gave them a standing ovation. Ira melted with embarrassment. She hoped that her children's or grandchildren's friends were not in the restaurant. She looked around. The dance had made her feel alive but now she felt anxious. Had she overstepped her freedom? Had she crossed a line?

Neither the spaghetti arrabiata nor her favourite smoked mackerel could lift her spirits after that. She ate the profiteroles in silence watching the cream flow out of the puffed pastry. It cut her off from the merriment around and she slipped into a state of being a daughter and a mother before this independent woman who could allow herself such liberties. Hadn't she lived by the adage 'duty before self'?

"A penny for your thoughts; where are you?" asked Nandu, tapping her on her shoulder. "Thank you for the dance. It was a treat after so many years. Should we not meet again soon?"

She was too overwhelmed by the evening to reply but managed politely, "Thank you. You are very kind."

Later that night, as she lay awake in bed, going over the dance, step by step, her spirits fell bit by bit. Her mind again relived the conversation she had held with herself over so many years. Thirty years, two months and twenty-two days since Tushar left her and the children, she had built fences around herself. Should she bring them down, at least now? Should she allow herself another dance of life?

Ira began to cry.

*Raised in Patna and Chennai, **Kala Priyadarshini** (Priyadarshini Sharma) studied science before turning to literature, and moved to Mumbai after marriage. After raising three children, managing the family tea business, and even launching her own popular tea café in Kochi, she went back to college to study journalism and to do her Master's in literature. She has been with The Hindu newspaper's Kochi bureau for the past 18 years.*

PEERING THROUGH THE MIST

Rajitha Menon

I switched off the engine, stepped out of the car and stretched myself. Driving in Mumbai during the rains is an extreme sport; by the time I started the ascent to Lonavala, my nerves were frayed. "I should have got Rohit, he is a better driver than me... No, stop it! Don't think about him," the monologue played in my head as I approached the small tea stall, situated a little away from the road. The smell of wet earth gave way to the heady aroma of strong, sweet tea and *bhajjis* frying in oil as I got closer. I asked for a cup of tea and then looked longingly at the golden brown spicy fritters heaped on the side. "Rohit wouldn't approve of these, so much oil..." I shook my head in irritation and defiantly ordered two.

Clutching a sticky glass and the piping hot *bhajjis*, I gingerly sat on the rickety bench in front of the shop. There were a couple of people milling around the place, clicking pictures against a stunning backdrop of the Sahyadri range, its verdant green visible even through a light mist. As I looked on, a guy in a brown leather jacket posed for a petite girl enthusiastically clicking away on her phone. "Rohit would have said..." I sighed and yielded, allowing thoughts of him to flood my brain.

Everyone experiences a life-changing incident at least once – it could be a solo trip, changing cities, the death of a close one or even getting a pet. Mine was meeting a person. Rohit and I were introduced at a party and we clicked from the first moment. There was so much in common – we were both South Delhi kids, new to Mumbai, street-food lovers and cricket enthusiasts. Within two weeks, we were inseparable; after a month, he proposed. I said yes even before he opened the box with the ring.

Everything was perfect; it seemed like I was living in a Bollywood fantasy. He got me flowers and chocolates. I cooked his favourite dishes. We went for movies and late-night drives. Our parents knew about us and were more than happy. But...

A burst of laughter jolted me out of my reverie. An old Omni had pulled up in front of the shop and a group of kids tumbled out of it. They were somewhat shabbily dressed but visibly excited. While they giggled at the couples around them and pointed at the mountains, a middle-aged lady climbed out of the driver's seat. She shepherded her wards towards the shop, where they asked for everything they could see. "Milk, biscuits, tea, chocolate, *bhajji*, *pakora*, Big Babool..." the list flowed free and fast. The shopkeeper gave his little customers a stern glare and looked doubtfully at the lady. She smiled and said, "Give them whatever they want. Once you are done, give me tea." Having been assured of his payment, the portly man relaxed a little and even allowed himself a little smile as he handed out the items. Clutching a small glass and instructing the children not to wander off too far, the lady came and sat next to me.

I looked at her surreptitiously. She was well-dressed and looked educated and was obviously a good enough driver to trust herself with that rickety van on high-range roads. Must be one of those NGO types, I thought to myself. Just then she glanced in my direction and smiled. I coloured (did she realise I was judging her?) and smiled back. "Is it raining on the top too?" she asked me.

"I don't know, ma'am, I am going up myself now."

"Oh, I see. With friends or...?"

"No one. I am going by myself," I said and prepared myself for the prying questions that I was sure would follow.

She looked at me closely. "Well, be careful. It seems to have rained heavily and the roads would be slippery. You seem quite tired; take care you don't doze off at the wheel."

I don't know what I was expecting to hear but it definitely wasn't this. The unexpected kindness from a rank stranger, the melancholy of a rainy morning and my own thoughts tugged at my heart and, to my horror, I found my eyes welling up.

"Oh, my dear, are you okay?" she enquired, her own eyes wide with concern.

"I am fine... Actually no, I am not. It's just been a rough couple of days recently and I... no, it's alright. I will be fine soon," I gulped and gave her a weak smile.

She gave me a piercing gaze, got up and walked over to the shop. Within a minute, she came back and pressed a Five Star into my hands. "I have always found that chocolate helps drown sorrow," she smiled. I took it gratefully but my heart gave a quick twinge. "I shouldn't be eating this. I am on a diet. My fiancé says I have put on too much weight lately."

"Nonsense. Anyone who says such things..." she scoffed and then quickly stopped.

"It's okay, I know what you were about to say," I said morosely.

"I don't mean to pry, *beta*, but if you want to eat something, you should," she patted me on my shoulder. I nodded and opened the chocolate wrapper, trying to swallow the lump in my throat with the chocolate. We sat in silence for some time.

"I am trying so hard to match his standards but it just seems impossible," I burst out vehemently, startling her; she obviously wasn't expecting me to continue our conversation. "Rohit is perfect, you know. School captain, college union president, basketball champion – you name it, he has done it. All my achievements seem to pale in front of him. If I talk about my solo trip to Goa, he tells me his experience of backpacking through Europe. If I do twenty sit-ups, he tells me he can do fifty. He helps my parents with their taxes and gives relationship advice to my friends. And each time, I feel so..." I stopped short with a sharp breath. "I am sorry, you don't want to hear all this," I said.

"That's quite alright," she looked at me kindly.

I kept quiet but I felt the words building up in my head. Why was I saying all this to her? 'Because she doesn't know Rohit and isn't going to say you are overthinking,' my brain reasoned. 'You need someone to just vent to, without offering any advice,' my heart added. My mouth obeyed.

"The only place where I feel I am doing something worthwhile is in my work. I really enjoy my job, and I have just got a six-month transition project in Germany. The day after I told him, he asked me to marry him. I mean, I love him but what's the hurry? Why is he so concerned about letting me go alone? I said, yes, of course. But I am not sure now. I mean I love him but... Mom thinks I am being selfish. My friends say he is a 'once-in-a-lifetime' man... The wedding is next month in Delhi. He is so excited and is spending a bomb on the arrangements but I am not able to feel happy," I blurted out, the words tumbling randomly as I rushed to finish my story before my audience decided to leave.

Silence again.

"What do you want to do?" she asked quietly.

Slightly in control of my faculties now, I shrugged. "Of course I want to be married. I mean, I love him. I guess I am overthinking, more opportunities will come along later."

"Maybe this is wedding panic," I giggled – only it came out as a high-pitched shriek that startled a couple nearby.

More silence. She had evidently decided not to say whatever was on her mind.

"So, what brings you here?" I attempted to lighten the mood.

"I had promised my students that whoever secures a distinction in the exams would get a trip to the mountains. They are not from very well-off families and had never been outside the city. So my bribe worked and here we are," she smiled fondly at the kids, some distance away.

"So you are a teacher?" This lady was continuously surprising me.

"Right now, yes. I was a VP in an F&O firm till two years back."

"Wow, that's quite a change!"

"Yes, all credit goes to my daughter," she smiled.

I kept quiet. If her daughter made her quit a well-paying cushy job in an MNC, which no doubt suited her qualifications, and made her attend to bratty kids in a slum, it was hardly a 'credit' to be proud of.

She looked over and grinned; I think she had an uncanny ability to guess what the other person was thinking. "My daughter was passionate about teaching. She was an IIT graduate but wanted to utilise her education to help underprivileged children. We fought bitterly over this but eventually, I let her have her way."

"Two years ago, while coming back after taking night classes for some kids, she met with an accident. Seems as if she dozed off at the wheel, tired after a hectic day."

The air around me suddenly grew stuffy and my breathing grew laboured. I understood the reason behind her concerned question earlier.

"She escaped but there was a head injury. The doctors gave her one year to live," the lady continued steadily. "We were all devastated but my daughter refused to bow out without a fight. She continued teaching, learned to play the guitar, got a tattoo and travelled extensively. One year, countless memories."

A brief pause.

"I quit my job to be with her, though she asked me not to. And as my daughter's life grew shorter, mine seemed meaningless. Colourless. I watched her interact with her students, laughing and glowing with life, and understood her insistence to do what she wanted. After she died, I couldn't bear to go back to a corporate job and continued teaching the children."

I bowed my head; I just couldn't take on more grief at the moment. "You did the right thing. We should do what we can for the people we love; they can be snatched away from us any moment," I whispered.

She startled me by laughing loudly. "Oh my God, is that what you took away from this story? You watch too many movies I think; they always tell the woman to be sacrificing in those. No, my dear, what I meant was that life is too short to do what is expected of you, you should do what you love. What makes you happy. Maybe it won't go as you planned but it will still be your plan. Your life. Your decisions," she smiled.

That was two hours ago. We spoke quite a bit, before exchanging names and numbers. I promised to visit her school before I left. She agreed to come to my farewell party. Then she took her Omni, gathered up the kids and drove on to the top. I stood there a bit, clicked a picture (the mountains really did look amazing), turned the car around and drove back. There was a lot of talking to be done and no time to lose. Anyway, I had wanted to go on a drive to clear my head and that did happen.

Remember what I said earlier? Everyone experiences a life-changing incident once in their life – it could be a solo trip, a change of place, the death of a close one or even getting a pet. Mine was meeting a person.

Rajitha Menon is a finance professional-turned-journalist who alternates between manic bursts of inspiration and extreme lethargy. Her choices in literature, music and movies are those with strong Indian influences. She is an alumnus of Asian College of Journalism and divides her time and loyalties between her hometown of Ernakulam in Kerala and Bengaluru, her adopted city.

THE TALKING HERON

Salini Vineeth

"Today, we are standing near this beautiful lake, thanks to one person's effort. He is a one-man army, an environmental superhero. Let me introduce Vasant, our special guest on this environmental day. His fearless fight with the garbage mafia saved this lake and its delicate ecosystem." The voice of the eloquent TV anchor boomed against the morning sky. It scared away the multitude of birds perched on the low branches around the lake. Curious joggers stopped by, seeing the camera.

The anchor gestured the cameraman to zoom in on Vasant.

"Good morning, Vasant. So, you are an engineer by profession, right? What inspired you to take up an environmental project?"

The anchor flashed a charming smile at the young man. Even though it was a cold January morning, Vasant sweated under the collective gaze of the crowd. It was all new to Vasant. He had never given an interview, let alone gone live on national television. After a social-media post about him went viral a few weeks ago, Vasant had got multiple media requests. While he could evade the others, this popular lifestyle channel was hell-bent on interviewing him.

Vasant blinked a few times at the camera, recollecting his answers. The channel had given him a set of questions a few days back. Even though the questions didn't resonate with him, Vasant spent hours preparing his answers. He was a straight-A student throughout his college, and he couldn't think of flunking an interview.

The anchor shot questions at Vasant with the grace and steadiness of a ballet dancer. Vasant nervously recited the practised answers. He took strategic pauses and deep breaths. The reassuring smile on the anchor's face told him that he was doing just fine. Ten questions later, Vasant was finally out of the misery. The anchor thanked him and shook his hand. The camera turned away from Vasant to pan over the serene lake.

"Pardon my intrusion, sir. What a poppycock interview that was! No heart at all!" A hoarse squawk startled Vasant. Flustered, he looked around. He was still standing next to the anchor, who was going on and on about the garbage issues and land mafia in the city. Vasant slipped away from the crowd and walked along the red-tiled walkway, eager to find the source of that strange voice.

"Hello, sir. Here, it's me. Look here." Vasant heard that voice again.

Leaning onto the peripheral railing of the lake, Vasant peeped into the water. Then he saw it. It was a beautiful heron! The bird stood delicately on a patch of water hyacinth, pecking on a lavender flower. Its white breast and reddish-brown wings perfectly contrasted its cyan-yellow beak.

It's not possible. A bird? Talking to me? Vasant wondered aloud. For a second, he thought that he was hallucinating again. During his darkest hours, he had had many such hallucinations.

"Oh, my dear sir, we most certainly can have a conversation. But I am afraid you humans have forgotten how to talk to birds!" With its long beak pointing at Vasant, the heron continued. Vasant looked around. The TV crew was on a boat, on their way to the islet in the middle of the lake. The onlookers had dispersed.

"I don't understand. What did you say? Umm... poppycock?"

"Sir, poppycock means nonsense. You were reciting a practised speech, and those TV schnooks didn't bother to ask you some real questions," the heron said.

"Again, what does schnook mean? I don't understand half of your words. But, how do you know that I was giving a practised speech?" Vasant asked. At some level, he was sure that it was just a dream. But he decided to play along. If it was a dream, it was a fantastic one for sure.

"Sir, I am an old-fashioned gentleman, if I do say so myself."

'A heron talking like a Victorian-era gentleman? I am either going insane or having a lucid dream!' Every second, this thought grew stronger in Vasant. Still, he couldn't help asking, "Why do you think the interview was nonsense?"

"I was perched on that high branch and was listening to you. Only your lips moved when you gave your little speech about, ah, what's that called? Umm... environmentalism. A heavy word I daresay! But sir, your heart was hither and thither, roaming around like a kite. Something is paining you. Am I justified in saying so?" the heron asked.

"Yeah, but how do you know?" A glass thread slowly started winding around Vasant's heart and it started bleeding again. It has been a long since he had a heart-to-heart with someone.

"That's quite simple, sir. Humans only pay attention to words. You only understand what is spoken out. We, birds, can interpret your gestures and even your silence," the heron beamed.

Vasant grew uneasy. He feared that his episodes of hallucination were coming back. It reminded him of the days when he would pump his veins full of chemicals and let himself float above the warm sea of intoxication. It was soon after she had left him.

"Dear, oh, dear! Sir, you are not hallucinating." The heron flapped its magnificent wings as if to wake Vasant from his musing. Vasant wanted to ask the heron how it had read his mind. But, he didn't bother to ask. Talking to a bird itself was strange enough. It may as well be a bird that could read minds. Vasant sniggered to himself, thinking about the weirdness of the situation.

"You winced when that pompous lady with the mic asked you about your inspiration. I could almost feel your pain," the heron continued. The smile on Vasant's face vanished in a second.

"You are right. It's painful to remember all that. I have never told anyone about her. No one has ever asked me." Vasant walked closer to the heron and sat on the walkway, his legs dangling in the lake.

"I am all ears. Pray tell more about it," the heron moved closer and perched on the railing. Vasant observed that it had kind eyes.

"There was someone whom I had surrendered my soul to. Until she came along, I didn't know that I was capable of so much love. My whole world shrank into her – her smile and the softness of her lips. Then she left me." Vasant clutched onto the metal railing. It was too cold and pained his palms.

"I am awfully sorry, sir. I shouldn't have shaken up the bitter memories." The heron bowed its head in an apology.

"No, no. It's okay. I can't say I am quite over her, but I have come to terms with the breakup. I realised there are more worthy things in life, like this lake. It helped me out of my addiction and saved my life," Vasant said. When he lovingly uttered "lake", a sense of satisfaction came over him.

"Oh, yes, dear sir. You have done a magnificent job! When I think about the past condition of this lake, I shiver in repulsion. The murky water and the stench of the garbage, good grief! We herons never came here. No self-respecting bird for that matter! It's only after I read an article about you in the newspaper that I came back to this lake. What a splendorous transformation!" the heron paused for a while.

"Do you read the newspaper? You are a strange bird!"

"Oh, I read everything that comes my way. I admire your bravery, sir! Driving off those pig-headed garbage thugs, that too single-handedly! I wonder where you got that courage!" the heron looked at Vasant with admiration.

A wan smile appeared on Vasant's face. Images of all those days flashed through his mind. Just before the lake had come into his life, he had really hit rock bottom. It was six months after his fiancée had broken up with him – alcohol and drugs reigned in his life.

"Soon after she left me, I reached my absolute low. I am not proud of the things I did during that time. I was about to take my life. It's on that day everything changed," Vasant gulped, remembering that night.

"Oh, heaven forbid, what would have happened if you had succeeded?" the heron asked. "Do continue, I apologise for the interruption,"

"It was her birthday. Even though she had broken up with me, I wanted to wish her. I called her many times, but she didn't pick up. I tried all day. By evening I was insane with grief and fury. I decided there was no point in living. So, I went to the balcony of my seventh-floor apartment that faced this lake. I stood there, shivering and crying. Suddenly, a wind blew from the lake carrying a rancid smell. It broke my nose. It was the garbage truck, stealthily unloading into the lake.

"I don't know what came over me. I ran out, started my Activa, and drove to this very place. It was a shabby place then. I asked those people to stop. They asked me to fuck off. Still, I tried to stop them, clicked a few photos. It enraged them. They beat me up real bad. I managed to come home. I was humiliated and furious. Surprisingly, I had forgotten all about her birthday. I think that was the moment that changed my life!" Vasant felt a bit breathless as he finished.

"So, was it just fury and humiliation that drove you?" heron asked in a grave tone.

"No, it was just a trigger, I guess. It suddenly reminded me of something that I had long forgotten – my closeness to nature. I was born in a hill-station in Kerala. I spent my childhood in the hills and helped my parents on our farm. Then I got into engineering. I was uprooted from the hills and replanted in this metro. I got lost in the chaos of this city. I stayed indoors, playing games, and spending time online. I had actually lost my connection with nature. The goons beating me up reminded me of what I had become. It was a slap on my face, quite literally, that bought me back to my senses," Vasant looked at the heron.

"Oh, that's the most extraordinary story I have ever heard. You have got quite a flair for poetry, my dear sir. I offer my gratitude, on behalf of all the birds in this lake. You have done us a great favour. Your selfless act has saved our habitat," the heron flapped its wings as if clapping its hands in appreciation.

"I can't say it was entirely selfless. When she left me, my world collapsed. Fighting for this lake gave me a purpose. It was not my work alone, as the TV channel said. There were people who treated me, helped me out of my addiction. There were people who worked with me on this campaign – kind souls who brought me back to life. I found solace in their company. I am not quite sure about the birds, but we humans need a sense of purpose and belongingness to live a meaningful life," Vasant paused and was briefly lost in reverie. The sun was climbing fast into the sky. The TV crew were back from their little picnic and were searching for Vasant.

"I must go now. It was nice talking to you," Vasant said with a smile. He no longer suspected that he was hallucinating.

"Oh, the pleasure was all mine, sir. Thank you for your most stimulating company. Allow me to take my leave." The heron bowed again and flew away gracefully.

"Vasant, who are you smiling at?" the TV anchor walked up to him and asked.

"I am thinking about things that humans fail to notice," Vasant said. His eyes were lost in the sky.

Salini Vineeth is a fiction and freelance writer based in Bengaluru. She worked for a decade in the electronics industry before turning to full-time writing. She has authored four books and has contributed to several anthologies and online magazines.

BE THE FLOW
Sangeetha Vallat

Asha sagged into the rickety chair, throwing a disapproving glance at her surroundings. A film of dust blanketed the shelves crammed with files and papers. She palpitated glancing at the multi-coloured flakes of paint peeling from the cracked walls and the ceiling that rained chalk on her whenever a train trundled past. Overgrown weeds snaked through the window, lavishly spreading tentacles aiming for the roof where a menacing fan rotated in slow motion. The artistic cobwebs in the four corners of the dingy room were to be her companions in her new office.

It was beyond her comprehension how a simple tiff with the ticketing supervisor could land her working shifts at the parcel office – a place where the faint-hearted feared to tread.

The parcel office, located on the farthest end of the platform, bustled with activity sixty minutes before the departure of trains and thirty minutes after their arrival. The rest of the day was entirely free, and she could walk to her quarters, a few strides away, sleep, read or carry out whatever activity fancied her.

A puny lady with a weathered face, old enough to be Asha's

grandmother, and a spirited young man with coiffured hair lingered in the room. The older lady wore a blue uniform sari; the man was in khakis.

"Madam, we are the parcel porters. Zahira Begum and myself Solomon." He flashed his white teeth and the Begum a grin that revealed multiple gaps.

"Okay. You guys also work in shifts?"

"Yes. Mostly I do the morning shift, and Begum comes in the evening."

"When was the last time somebody cleaned this place?"

"Last *Ayudha Puja*. The next one is in a couple of months."

"What is that disgusting stench?" asked Asha, her face contorted.

"Oh, those are the butter tins. *Uthukuli* butter is very famous." Solomon was crestfallen at Asha's ignorance.

"Hmm, I am not sure how everything works here. I hope you two will guide me. First, clean up this place; this dust will kill me."

"But madam, Goddess Lakshmi resides here, we shouldn't disturb her."

Asha grew exasperated listening to Solomon's 'wisdom'. Then she resigned to her fate; it wouldn't be possible to deliver swift changes in a system that had prevailed for years. She hoped to sweet-talk her way back to the ticketing office within a few weeks.

She listened attentively as Begum and Solomon brought her up to speed on the intricacies of what was expected of her in the parcel office.

"What? No! I don't take bribes," Asha gasped.

"Madam, everyone has to take a bribe. That's the unwritten rule here. I will deal with everything. You should tell the customer, 'Do as the porter says'. Rest assured, you will do fine here."

"But bribery is punishable. It's not right."

"Madam, the system is corrupt. You cannot change it. You are here for just a few months until you go back to the ticketing office. Just go with the flow."

Educated consequently, with the tariff for different 'items' of parcels, Asha opened up shop. Her first customer marched in with a consignment to parcel.

Asha carefully prepared the bill based on the details in the consignment form tendered by the customer. Accepting the payment for the bill, she handed over the receipt to the customer and a copy to the porter to wrap with the package.

Asha realised that she had forgotten to utter the magic words when Solomon signalled by clearing his throat.

"Err, do as the porter tells you," she muttered with a bent head.

The day was intermittently busy, with the delivery of more smelly butter tins and a booking of hundreds of day-old chicks, the cheeping of which resonated in the room and irritated Asha. The parcels that everyone looked forward to, however, were the rubber rolls. Neatly packed in gunny sacks, the rubber rolls – which were sent from rubber estates from Kerala to various industries around India – were considered gold mines in some railway stations.

Whenever a train brought in rubber rolls for delivery, the parcel office would see an influx of people who thronged to catch the action. Asha was surprised when she emerged from her room to receive the parcel load from the train and to sign the forms extended by the train's guard. The clerk and the porter on duty attracted envious looks; it was no secret that they would be going home with a bulky wallet at the end of their shift!

Every day at the end of her shift, Solomon handed over her 'share' of the day's earnings. Thrilled, Asha put her initial qualms to rest and walked home with a spring in her step. The days and weeks compounded into months, and with *Ayudha Puja* round the corner, the air was festive.

One day, a peasant approached Asha with a strange commodity. Pigs! Yes, he had ten squealing piglets on a leash. One amongst them turned rogue, scurried out of the parcel office and began romping about on the platform. Luckily, there were no trains at that time, and Asha and Begum pounced on the errant piglet and managed to capture it after a short, breathless chase. For the next few nights, Asha was haunted by nightmares – the squealing piglets escaped her grasp every time.

Asha gradually settled in her role as the parcel clerk. Solomon regaled her with anecdotes of the parcel booking office, and Begum entertained her by singing old Hindi *ghazals*.

Little did Asha know that soon an episode involving her would be written in the annals of 'parcel office' history.

**

Asha's fiancé visited her at work one day and was appalled at her working conditions. Asha brushed aside his concerns and informed him of the 'money-minting' game. This petrified him, and he gave her an earful of the risks involved in accepting a bribe.

"Promise me that you will never do that."

Sullenly, Asha acquiesced, adding, "But give me time, I will wean off it slowly, and I cannot stop the porters from earning extra money."

He was infuriated with her careless flippancy. Finally, Asha promised to resist the blatant charm of easy money.

The next day, Asha was ordered to attend to the parcel office at the next station. The clerk there was taken ill suddenly, and Asha had to cover his shift. The supervisor would work the shift at her station. This was a common practice where the junior staff worked as 'rest givers' in a section of the railways.

Asha boarded the earliest train to be in time for work.

The parcel office in the next station appeared no different than her own: the same peeling paint, broken chair and cobwebs. The porter Narasaiah was a one-eyed man in khakis. He was gruff and reluctant to warm up to her. Asha missed her Begum and Solomon.

A string of customers waited to book parcels. They kept Asha busy during the first half of the day. She strolled around the station post-lunch, where she witnessed a harrowing incident.

She recognised the scrawny woman who had come in earlier to book a parcel of books to send to her daughter who was in college in the neighbouring state. Asha had pitied her appearance, more so when the woman took out small change to pay the bill. The others waiting to book parcels murmured in irritation. The lady trembled and fumbled, which led to the coins scattering all over the room further delaying the other customers.

Asha presently witnessed Narasaiah haggling with the same woman, who was now sobbing and imploring. Before Asha could intercede, she was summoned to the station manager's cabin to discuss the duty roster.

As the rest of the day moved at a snail's pace, Asha pondered over the episode and was ashamed of her colleague's behaviour. The realisation that a share of money thus earned had been oiling her wheels too distressed and mortified her immensely.

With an hour to end her shift, Asha called the porter.

The one-eyed porter squatted on the floor and handed Asha some soiled currency.

"Madam, your share."

"No, Narasaiah, I won't accept a bribe. You can keep it. It is all yours."

Narasaiah's face blossomed into a smile.

"You are almost as old as my father. I am embarrassed to talk to you like this. I am no saint. I know how this all works, and I also know I can't stop you from accepting a bribe. But can I request you not to demand extra money from poor people? That lady with the parcel of books was pleading. I saw it."

"Madam, sorry. I have three daughters to wed," grumbled Narasaiah, scratching his head.

With a sigh, she measured her words, but they were disturbed by a customer.

Asha had already tallied the accounts and was annoyed to tend to a customer at closing time. Mechanically, she drew up the receipt and collected the cash.

"The petrol tank should be dry; the porter will do the needful packing."

Asha was in a hurry to catch the train home. She announced to Narasaiah that he should finish up the packing and lock the office, and that she would remit the day's collection at the booking office and board the next train.

Within a few minutes of Narasaiah walking out with the customer, seven men marched inside with Narasaiah amidst them. Asha was perplexed. It looked like a hostage situation in the movies.

A tall man addressed her in an authoritative voice, flashing an identity card, "Madam, we are vigilance officers. We received complaints about the parcel clerk, and this is a surprise check. We caught your porter red-handed trying to bargain a bribe."

Asha turned deathly pale. She staggered and held on to the desk as the man continued, "Please cooperate with us. We need to check your accounts and tally your day's earnings. First, please show us how much personal cash you have and bring the personal-cash register that you had declared before you commenced your shift."

Asha hastily showed them the books, and the men meticulously checked the registers. This was a well-planned operation. Thanking her fiancé inwardly, she signed the letter proffered by the vigilance officers, which certified, "Accounts and personal cash tallied without any discrepancy."

A young officer was chatty, "Your signature is shaky. The clerk must have received a tip-off, that's why he feigned illness and you were called for duty. Lucky that you are principled and not corrupt."

Asha managed a wan smile. Her insides were churning, and she excused herself to go to the washroom and retched. She remembered her fiancé's words, "Everything has a domino effect; your casual demands of bribery and nonchalance might have dangerous repercussions on everybody around you." She shuddered imagining being cuffed and taken away and dismissed from service ingloriously.

Things did not go well for the porter. He was booked on charges of corruption and placed under immediate suspension from work. Asha boarded the last train, head held high. A timely correct decision had saved her career and life.

She appeared as a witness for the defendant in the trial that ensued in the vigilance office a few weeks later. Narasaiah had only a few months of service left until retirement; Asha's little assistance could save his pension, informed the lawyer appointed by the staff welfare union.

Asha never received another dime besides her remuneration from the government.

She didn't stay in the parcel office for long, nor did she work anymore shifts in the booking office. Cement bags currently surround Asha. A bandana partly covers her face in feeble protection against the cement dust and the lure of large kickbacks. Steeling herself to 'stay clean', she is furiously calculating wharfage in the goods shed – a frowzier but wealthier place than the parcel office.

Sangeetha Vallat *had a memorable career spanning 14 years in the Indian Railways after which she opted for voluntary retirement. She now spends her time surrounded by books. She picked up writing recently after the demise of her father as a way of dealing with grief, and has warned friends and family that they may end up in some form in her stories.*